"What is it?" Christina hated the shaky quality of her voice.

Dylan placed his hand gently on her shoulder. "Come on. We can call the sheriff. Then have your car towed."

"No, I need to see." Christina brushed past him and peered through the hole in the driver's side window. Shards of glass dangled from the hole, waiting for gravity to drop them to the ground.

She blinked a few times, trying to process the scene. Her vision narrowed and tiny dots danced in her line of vision. Whoever did this didn't leave a note. Instead, they had left a large knife sticking out of her headrest.

Christina turned around, squaring her shoulders. Steeling her spine. "Who would do this?" Had Roger already made good on his promise to make her sorry if she caused trouble?

The look of compassion on Dylan's face weakened her resolve. She wasn't used to relying on anyone. "What's going on?" she asked, her voice shaky.

"We're going to find out. And I won't let you out of my sight until we do."

Alison Stone lives with her husband of more than twenty years and their four children in Western New York. Besides writing, Alison keeps busy volunteering at her children's schools, driving her girls to dance and watching her boys race motocross. Alison loves to hear from her readers at Alison@AlisonStone.com. For more information, please visit her website, alisonstone.com. She's also chatty on Twitter, @alison_stone. Find her on Facebook at Facebook.com/alisonstoneauthor.

Books by Alison Stone

Love Inspired Suspense

Plain Pursuit
Critical Diagnosis
Silver Lake Secrets
Plain Peril
High-Risk Homecoming
Plain Threats
Plain Protector
Plain Cover-Up

PLAIN COVER-UP

ALISON STONE

HARLEQUIN® LOVE INSPIRED® SUSPENSE

Recycling programs
for this product may
not exist in your area.

 LOVE INSPIRED BOOKS

ISBN-13: 978-0-373-44761-9

Plain Cover-Up

www.Harlequin.com

Printed in U.S.A.

You are my hiding place;
You will protect me from trouble
and surround me with songs of deliverance.
–*Psalms* 32:7

To Scott, Scotty, Alex, Kelsey & Leah.
Love you guys always and forever.

ONE

The gathering storm clouds hastened nightfall's arrival. In the distance, lightning split the sky. Christina groaned. If she hadn't been so swamped at the healthcare clinic, she might have taken a second to check the weather forecast and realized a more prudent decision would have involved driving to the Apple Creek Diner for takeout versus walking the half mile.

A gust of wind whipped up and rustled through the trees, thick with green foliage after a harsh northern winter. The air was heavy with the expectation of rain. Dr. Christina Jennings wrapped the plastic handle of the takeout bag around her wrist and quickened her pace. The thought of getting drenched when she still had hours of paperwork to do in the clinic was about as appealing as, well, dealing with the paperwork itself.

As the soft footsteps of her tennis shoes sounded on the pavement, fingers of awareness kneaded the back of her neck and she resisted the urge to glance back at the diner. No doubt Dylan Hunter had a perfect view of her on the street from his window booth when she left the diner. She refused to let this man occupy her thoughts. A man who had broken her heart in two.

Christina's stomach growled, snapping her focus back to the purpose of her short break from work. The thought of the BLT sandwich in the bag dangling off her wrist made her walk even faster. She was *so* hungry.

Georgia Summers, the newly hired physician assistant at the clinic, often joked that Christina probably would never stop working if she could find a way to function on no food and zero sleep. The sleep she sacrificed, food, not so much. Christina smiled at the memory of Georgia's laugh. It was nice to have someone to work with after running the clinic by herself for so many years.

With her free hand, Christina pulled her light jacket closed and fastened the zipper at the bottom. A shudder twined its way up her spine, making her feel unsettled.

Had chatting with Dylan for a few moments at the diner really thrown her *this* off balance?

Christina had carefully avoided him since he moved to Apple Creek earlier in the year to teach at the law school. She still had no idea why he was on leave from the FBI, his self-proclaimed dream job. And frankly she didn't care. She figured he had lost interest and moved onto his next thing, much like he had done with her. Maybe he'd go back. Maybe he wouldn't.

But tonight she'd had no choice but to make small talk with him because the diner was empty and Flo, the long-time waitress, took a while to pull her order together. If Christina had been suspicious by nature, she'd have thought Flo's delay had been intentional.

What doesn't kill you will make you stronger. Franny's favorite expression floated to mind. Well, one of many favorite expressions of her parents' housekeeper.

A deep rumble of thunder sounded in the distance. Maybe she should have taken the ride Dylan had offered.

She probably would have taken the offer if it had come from *anybody* else.

Christina hustled past the stores on Main Street to the residences with postage-stamp-size lawns. She used to rent one of these apartments, until she'd realized she wanted a more rural setting where she could have privacy.

Cigarette smoke wafted in her direction. Instinctively, she turned to see where it was coming from, but could only see the red glow of a cigarette in the shadows. Feeling like she was being watched, she squared her shoulders and walked with an air of authority.

Don't walk like a victim.

The notion that a victim somehow asked for it by acting a certain way made her bristle. However, being aware of one's surroundings was always a good idea. A college student had been attacked in the nearby apartments a couple of weeks ago.

Christina had treated the woman for minor injuries, including a superficial knife wound across her cheek. Thank goodness the young woman had gotten away, but Christina and her brother, Deputy Nick Jennings, worried the attacker might grow bolder. The woman couldn't identify whoever had assaulted her, and any leads had dried up.

Maybe that's where Christina's apprehension stemmed from. It had everything to do with a recent attack and nothing to do with seeing Dylan Hunter again.

Christina kept her steady pace, refusing to live in fear.

Been there, done that.

However, there was something to be said about being smart. Safe. Christina walked more briskly, ignoring the whisper of dread sending goose bumps across her flesh.

A gust of wind picked up and whipped loose strands

of hair across her face. She hooked a piece of hair with her free hand and dragged it out of her mouth. Even though they were a month away from the official start of summer, a storm could sweep in and drop the temperature by ten or even twenty degrees. All she had on was a light jacket.

A fat drop of rain hit her head. Christina held up her palm to confirm what her head already knew. With her free hand, she flipped up the hood on her spring jacket.

Christina untwisted the plastic bag from around her wrist, fearing it was cutting off the circulation to her tingling fingers. She switched hands and focused on the crunching of the gravel under her feet as she turned onto the country road. The healthcare clinic was only a hundred yards or so away, across the street from some ball fields. If she hurried, she'd make it before the skies opened up.

Too late.

The intermittent drops turned into a wall of torrential rain. Holding her jacket closed with both hands—the bag dangling from her hand—Christina ran toward the clinic with her head down. Her dinner in the plastic bag banged against the tops of her thighs. Already she lamented the demise of her sandwich.

The slam of a car door made Christina glance up. The headlights of a sedan parked in front of the clinic blinded her. She squinted against the brightness, the rain peppering her face. Unease slid its way up her spine.

Heart thundering in her chest, she raced toward the car. Perhaps someone had had an emergency. She waved to them in case they had come looking for her and found the clinic locked. Christina had told Georgia to leave if she needed to and to put a sign on the door that the physician would be right back.

As Christina got closer to the vehicle, the hairs on her arms prickled to life as if charged by an electrical storm. The pounding of rain on the metal gutters of the nondescript building mingled with her frantic heartbeat. The car's tires spun before gaining traction in the gravel parking lot.

Christina dropped her takeout bag and waved her arms frantically. Maybe they couldn't see her in the rain. The car covered the ground between them. Christina froze for the briefest of seconds before she saw a dark form bearing down on her out of the corner of her eye.

Christina closed her eyes tight as she was shoved sideways and a man landed on top of her. Her shoulder hit the ground with a resounding thud. She groaned. The sound of gravel churning close to her head sent terror racing through her heart.

Shivering with icy panic, Christina opened her eyes a fraction and saw Dylan Hunter staring down at her. "You okay?"

"I…um…" Christina shifted her head to see the rain and dusk swallowing up the taillights of the vehicle that had officially ruined her evening.

Dylan rolled off her and stood. He held out his hand to help her up, his gaze locked on the departing car. Her wet hair whipped against her face. Before she had time to mourn the loss of her BLT—now scattered across the gravel—she acknowledged her gratitude.

Thank you, Lord, for protecting me from that car. For keeping me safe.

Getting to her feet, her hand still in his solid grasp, she shook her head in disbelief. "What in the world…?"

"I was only able to get a partial plate. It's something. And he had a busted taillight," Dylan bit out between breaths.

Where had Dylan come from?

It was then that she noticed his truck and the driver's side door yawning open on the side of the road, as if he had arrived just in time to push her out of the way.

Something drew her attention to the front door of the clinic. In the dim light of the bulb on the overhang, she saw a heap of fabric. Renewed fear zinged through her system, immediately making her forget about her near-death experience.

Christina yanked her hand out of Dylan's and ran toward the door. As she approached, she recognized the traditional Amish dress, boots and bonnet.

Her pulse spiked. "Naomi!" The young Amish woman, now curled up by the brick wall of the clinic, cleaned her office twice a week.

"Naomi," Christina said again, this time more urgently. She touched the young woman's face and her head lolled back, her eyes closed. Christina glanced over her shoulder and yelled to Dylan who was only steps away, "Help me get her into the clinic."

With wet, cold, shaky fingers, Christina struggled to dig her keys out of the back pocket of her jeans, all the while repeating a prayer for poor Naomi. The metal key skidded across the lock before Christina was able to insert it into the slot and unlock the door.

Christina pushed the door wide for Dylan and pressed herself firmly against it as he carried her Amish friend over the threshold like a bride. "Follow me to the back exam room."

Christina strode down the narrow hallway, slapping

at light switches as she went. Her heartbeat jackhammered, her body's automatic response to an emergency. It had served her well as a physician. Her brother always laughed at her and told her she would have been good in times of war. But that had been his gig.

Hers was helping people who couldn't afford healthcare.

Hers was saving lives.

"Back here," Christina repeated unnecessarily as Dylan strode down the hall right behind her, carrying Naomi. The young woman's head flopped against Dylan's chest. Christina willed Naomi to open her eyes. Respond to them. Respond to something.

Christina reached the first exam room and pushed open the door. It bounced off the wall with a force she hadn't intended. She reached in and flipped the last switch. The fluorescent bulbs flickered and buzzed to life. One of these days she'd have to replace these migraine-inducing lights, but she hated to ask her parents for additional funds that didn't go directly toward patient care.

Despite her parents' wealth and generosity, funds weren't unlimited. They had drilled that into her when she was a little girl. The Jenningses understood the value of money and what it could achieve. People had to be good stewards of their blessings. And, like on most everyone else, the economy had been tough on Jennings Enterprises.

Christina shuffled out of the way and grabbed her stethoscope from the hook. Dylan laid Naomi down on the crinkly paper covering the table. Christina found a steady pulse and breathed a sigh of relief.

"Grab a blanket from the top shelf in the closet in

the hallway," she commanded Dylan without turning to look at him.

He slipped out of the room.

"Hello, hello… Naomi." Christina patted the young woman's cheek. "You're at the healthcare clinic with Dr. Christina… You're safe."

"Here, I have the blanket and I found some dry clothes in the same closet," Dylan said as he burst back into the room. He moved with the efficiency of a man who was good at dealing with emergencies. The FBI had probably instilled that in him.

"Thank you."

Dylan unfolded the blanket and placed it over the Amish woman. "You know her?"

Christina nodded. "Yes, she does some light cleaning for me here at the clinic a few days a week. Her name's Naomi Mullet. I've gotten to know her because I'm usually still working when she arrives to clean."

The young woman stirred and Christina snapped her attention back to her patient and placed a comforting hand on her arm. "You're safe, Naomi. It's Dr. Christina."

Dylan pulled his cell phone out of his back pocket. "I'll call the sheriff."

"Neh…neh…" The Amish woman muttered, her voice groggy.

"You're safe," Christina repeated. She brushed the back of her knuckles across Naomi's cool cheek— Christina would have to get her to change into the dry clothes—and watched as Naomi struggled to open her eyes a fraction.

The woman strained against the blanket and Christina put her hand on her shoulder to reassure her. "Take it easy. You're safe. You're at the clinic."

"No police. Please. And don't tell my *mem* and *dat*." Naomi's voice was racked with panic as she gained awareness of her surroundings.

Christina nodded, understanding Naomi's aversion to the police, but not sure why she wouldn't want her parents notified. As far as the police went, the Amish customarily preferred to deal with things on their own.

However, someone had hurt Naomi and dumped her at the clinic's front door. This was the second woman who had been injured in Apple Creek in recent weeks. Christina's mind immediately jumped to the first logical thought: *were the assaults connected?* It seemed a stretch, yet both women were rendered unconscious and things like this didn't often happen in the small town.

But Naomi's panicked expression gave Christina pause. Calling the sheriff would have to wait. Naomi's well-being came first. Maybe she could convince the young Amish woman later, once she had a chance to clear her head. Christina had to swallow the anger simmering below the surface. Not only for this woman, but for the other victim and a younger version of herself. A younger version who had been too afraid to accuse her attacker. A younger version who had also chosen to remain silent.

Christina brushed her hand across her face and forced away the thought. She studied Dylan, hoping he hadn't noticed her moment of weakness.

"Hold off on making any calls." Christina's tone was far calmer than the emotions rioting inside her. She wanted to find whoever had dumped her dear friend off and nearly run over her. She wanted to find him and... She shook away the less-than-Christian thoughts.

Christina had to find justice for this young woman, her friend, one way or another. Over the years, Christina had taken pride in helping a handful of abused women escape their abusers and create new lives elsewhere.

The adrenaline surging through her veins was making her thoughts race out of control. She didn't even know what happened to Naomi, yet. Maybe Christina had completely misread the situation.

Naomi struggled to sit up, her bonnet askew on her head. Christina held Naomi's arm and helped her to a sitting position. She stood close, watching Naomi for any signs that she was going to pass out or be sick. She conducted a few tests to check for a concussion. Christina suspected the young woman had been drugged. The normally chatty Amish woman's eyes were wide with fear. A tremble seemed to ripple through her when she locked gazes with Dylan.

Understanding better than most, Christina smiled apologetically at Dylan. "Can you give us privacy for a minute?"

"Sure." Unspoken understanding stretched between them. "I'll be in the hallway."

"And Dylan," Christina added, *"don't* call the sheriff."

The Amish woman gasped in relief. *"Denki." Thank you.*

The door clicked closed and Christina turned back to the young woman. "Naomi, who did this to you?"

Naomi averted her eyes and shook her head. *"Neh."*

"What happened?"

Silence.

"You can trust me. I'll help you." Christina brushed her fingers along a tender bruise on the young woman's cheek. Naomi flinched.

"I don't know."

Christina took a steadying breath. "You don't have to

be afraid." A memory never far from the surface weighed on Christina's lungs. With determination, she focused on what was right in front of her. Naomi. Her patient. Christina could help her.

Christina had always focused on what was right in front of her. Her education. Her career. Never deviating from the path.

It's what kept her sane.

Naomi looked up and fear flickered across her face. "I went to a barn party with a friend." She blinked slowly. "I don't remember much else."

Christina clasped her hands in front of her, suspecting Naomi was intentionally being evasive. However, she feared Naomi had been drugged. Perhaps someone had spiked her drink. Or maybe she had been unaccustomed to drinking and had overdone it?

"Have you been drinking?" Christina cringed at the unintended accusation in her tone. Even if Naomi had been drinking, she didn't deserve to be attacked and dumped like yesterday's garbage in a parking lot.

Christina's mind flashed back to her college roommate's accusatory tone when Christina began to relate her own story after an incident with a man she had trusted.

Are you sure you weren't a tease? I can't believe he'd do that to you. He's such a nice guy. And a friend of your brother's. He has a wife and kid. Why would he attack you?

As if any of those reasons would stop a predator. As if her roommate's disbelief and uncertainty had made what happened to Christina less real. Despite the unease quivering in her stomach, Christina placed her hand on Naomi's shoulder. "Even if you did drink, you didn't deserve to get attacked."

"One beer," Naomi said, her voice hoarse. The Amish woman studied her clenched hands in her lap, shame radiating from her hunched posture. "I didn't plan to drink. I wanted…" Her voice trailed off as if she was carefully measuring how much to reveal.

Christina had been drinking the night she was attacked. Perhaps too much.

A night of hazy memories and accusations.

"Naomi, you can trust me. I'll do whatever I can to help you. Tell me what you remember."

The Amish woman tugged at a blue and purple yarn bracelet on her wrist, such a small thing but it showed she was straddling two worlds. "I told you everything I remember."

"Who brought you here?" Christina asked, trying to coax out the answers Naomi was holding back.

Naomi shrugged. A single tear trailed down her cheek. "It's all so fuzzy. Where did you find me?"

"Outside in the rain." Christina tilted her head to study the young woman. A deep line creased Naomi's forehead as if they were discussing someone else altogether.

"You don't remember?"

Naomi shook her head again. "My *Englisch* friend Cheryl brought me to the party, but I lost track of her." Her eyes flashed wide. "It wonders me if something happened to her." Naomi's entire body trembled and her lower lip had turned a disconcerting shade of blue.

"Is Cheryl the friend who sometimes drives you to work?"

"*Yah.* Do you know where she is?"

Christina placed her hand on Naomi's arm. "We'll find out. First I need you to change into this gown for an exam."

"Neh, neh..." Naomi fisted the fabric of her dress at her chest. She shook her head and what little color she had in her cheeks visibly drained.

"You have a right to refuse any exam, but if someone hurt you," Christina spoke softly so as not to further spook her young Amish friend, "we need to collect evidence."

"Neh, I don't want anyone to know. Please."

Christina's heart broke for the young woman and she fought to remain calm. She patted the sweatpants and sweatshirt sitting on the exam table. "Would you give me a urine sample? It would help us determine the drugs in your system. You can use the bathroom right there."

"I didn't take drugs. I don't do drugs."

"Someone could have slipped you something in a drink."

"I only had one beer." Naomi bowed her head. "I shouldn't have had that."

"No, one's blaming you." Christina smiled. "I'd like to do a test to check."

Naomi seemed hesitant at first, then agreed.

"Okay, then. Take care of the sample, then change into these dry clothes. We'll chat once you're dry."

"You're not going to call the sheriff?"

Again, Christina carefully phrased her reply. "No, not unless you agree. I believe we should, but I'll respect your wishes." She smiled again, trying to reassure Naomi that she could trust her. "Take care of this—" she tapped the specimen container "—then get dressed."

Naomi looked up at her with trusting eyes and Christina worried that she wasn't worthy of such confidence. Such trust. Trust she had repeatedly sought from other victimized women who had come through her clinic over the years.

It was a long road.

Christina had failed miserably in protecting herself. She had allowed one night—one man—to define her. To shape her choices.

But would helping Naomi put Christina in harm's way? Had it already? Christina touched her arm, tender from landing hard on it when Dylan pushed her out of the path of the racing car.

None of that mattered. She had to help Naomi.

Christina patted Naomi's hand, making a silent promise that she'd protect the woman. To help her not let tonight define who she was.

Dear God, help me do right by this young woman.

TWO

Dylan drummed his fingers on the counter-height surface outside of the exam room in the rear of the Apple Creek Healthcare Clinic. He understood the young Amish woman's need for privacy, but he was eager to learn who had dropped her off at the clinic because that same person tried to run Christina over with his vehicle.

It didn't make sense. Someone cared enough to drop Naomi off here, but had recklessly aimed their vehicle at the physician meant to help her. Clearly whoever it was wasn't thinking. Period.

Or perhaps they hadn't realized the figure walking toward them was the physician. Either way, they were reckless and needed to be found.

The cold fingers of dread scraped across the back of his neck. What if he hadn't hopped into his truck to see if Christina needed a ride with the approaching storm? She had refused his offer at the diner, and she could be stubborn. She had proven that by giving him the cold shoulder ever since he moved back to Apple Creek in January. Five months of polite greetings on the street. Nothing more. Nothing less.

He supposed he deserved that. He had broken up with

Christina when they were both at Genwego State. She'd been an undergraduate and he was finishing up law school. He had told her he wanted to move to Buffalo to be an FBI agent and had no plans of settling down, least of all in Apple Creek. The breakup had been both efficient and cruel.

But life had a way of getting back at him, dishing out a hearty helping of cruelty. Now here he was serving as an interim professor at his alma mater, on extended leave from the FBI. He hadn't been the kind of agent he had hoped to be, and his partner, Special Agent Nora Reed, had paid the ultimate price. And when an opening came up at the law school, he figured, why not? It gave him something to do besides ruminate over his failings.

Dylan shook his head, trying to dispel the dark clouds forever hovering over him. He paced the small space outside the three exam rooms, eager to expend his restless energy, eager to hear Naomi's version of events. He rubbed the back of his neck, grateful that tonight he *had* been in the right place at the right time. Christina had nearly been run over. His childhood self might have thanked God for the act of divine intervention, but his tough upbringing didn't give him many opportunities to thank anyone, let alone God.

The floorboards creaked behind the closed door and Dylan watched the door handle turn. Christina appeared, directing Naomi to the bathroom. When Dylan started to ask Christina what was going on, she shook her head. A few minutes later, Naomi emerged, holding wet garments and looking like any other teen fresh out of the shower, with wet hair and comfy clothes.

"Everything okay?" he asked.

Christina opened her mouth to say something when

the front door crashed open. "Hello?" a female's voice hollered down the hall. "Hello, I'm looking for Naomi Mullet. Is Naomi here?" The young woman sounded strained as she drew closer.

Recognition dawned on Naomi's face, with a hint of relief. "Cheryl." Naomi moved toward her friend's voice and stumbled over a lump in the carpet. Dylan grabbed her elbow to steady her.

Christina pushed a chair over. "Sit here. I'll bring Cheryl back."

Naomi nodded, relief and exhaustion playing on her pretty face.

Cheryl charged into the back of the clinic dressed in blue jeans and a university sweatshirt. Her red hair was pulled into a long ponytail, her freckles prominent on her pale skin. Relief lit her heavily made-up eyes. "There you are! I was *so* worried." She gave her Amish friend's sweatpants and sweatshirt a once over. "What happened to your clothes?"

Christina watched the young woman intently. "Were you at the party with Naomi?" To Christina's credit, there was no hint of blame or accusation in her voice. During his law enforcement career, Dylan noticed adults tended to blame teens first, ask questions second.

"Yes." Cheryl's lips quivered. "I drove her to the party. Naomi didn't plan on staying." A smile touched the corners of her glossed lips. "Usually when Naomi used to go to parties with me she tried to fit in."

"You mean, she didn't wear her Amish clothes?" Dylan asked, slipping into FBI interrogation mode.

"No, she didn't. She'd dress casual. Like me. I'm not Amish." Cheryl giggled nervously. "Lots of Amish kids break the rules. They're trying to figure things out."

"You've heard of *Rumspringa*?" Naomi spoke up. "I lost my way for a little while. I did things—" her voice cracked "—I'm not proud of. But I'm determined to live the Amish Way."

"Then why go to the party?" Christina asked, studying the young Amish woman with her intense brown eyes.

"I heard Lloyd Burkholder was supposed to be there. I needed to talk to him." Naomi groaned. "Please tell me he didn't show up."

Cheryl shrugged. "I don't know. I was talking to some friends outside the barn. By the time I went in, I couldn't find you. Someone told me you didn't feel well and Ben Reist was taking you to the clinic."

"Ben?" Naomi's eyebrows drew together. "I sort of remember. Maybe not…" She bit her lower lip. "Does he have short blond hair?" She touched her own head for emphasis.

Excitement drummed in Dylan's veins. They had a possible name for the driver who nearly ran Christina over.

"What kind of kid is Ben Reist?" Dylan asked, his tone harsher than he intended. Naomi looked like a scared rabbit and he didn't want her to dart.

Cheryl laughed, a sound void of humor. "Good kid. I was surprised he was at the party. Not really the partying kind."

"Do you think he meant to hurt me?" All that Naomi's question didn't ask tore at Dylan.

"No way. Ben's a good guy. Someone said he could tell you seemed out of it and he wanted to get you out of there." Cheryl's eyes grew wide. "As soon as I heard, I jumped into the car. I figured you had too much to drink. The party was getting out of control anyway. All the kids were bailing. They were kinda freaked that the sheriff would show up once some underage drunk Amish girl was dropped at the healthcare clinic."

"I believe she may have drugs in her system," Christina said, matter-of-factly.

"Drugs?" Cheryl's voice cracked.

"I didn't take drugs." Naomi said without much conviction. "I only had a beer. And I don't remember finishing it. Dr. Christina thinks someone could have put something in my drink."

Dylan watched Naomi closely for signs she wasn't telling the truth.

"Does that seem about right to you, Naomi?" Christina asked.

"It makes sense." Naomi's eyes got a faraway look. She glanced at the clock. "I wasn't there that long and then everything went fuzzy."

A hint of relief settled into the soft lines around Christina's eyes. They both must have been thinking the same thing. The time frame didn't likely allow for a sexual assault. This Ben Reist kid had ushered Naomi out of there before whoever drugged her drink had had a chance to act.

"If Ben is such a nice guy, why didn't he stick around to make sure Naomi was okay?" Dylan ran through the events in his mind, including the fact that Christina had nearly been run over.

Cheryl shrugged. "Probably didn't want to get into trouble. Kids don't always think." She said it in a way that made him wonder how old she was. "I hear he's got a scholarship to some big university starting in the fall. I imagine he didn't want to jeopardize that. Rumor has it he was in trouble with the police earlier this year. He can't get in trouble again."

Dylan shook his head, frustrated at the dumb decisions kids sometimes made.

Christina gathered Naomi's wet clothes. "I'm going to run these through the wash."

Dylan pulled her aside. "Is that…?" He wanted to ask if that was a good idea. That the clothes might serve as evidence, but he could tell by the look on Christina's face that she had already waged and lost that battle with the young Amish girl. Even in the case of a possible sexual assault, in New York State the victim had the right to refuse evidence collection. And if Cheryl was to be believed, Ben had brought Naomi straight from the party to the clinic, minimizing the opportunity for such an assault.

His lips thinned and he gave Christina a quick nod.

Christina grabbed Dylan's arm and pulled him down the hall toward the laundry. She leaned in close and whispered, "I fear sending this sweet girl home in a dirty dress or sweatpants will create far more questions than she's willing to answer. I think we need to get her cleaned up and see her safely home."

Dylan nodded, sensing Christina was searching for his agreement.

Christina stepped away from Dylan and they returned to where the young women were standing. "The laundry's in the back. We'll wash your dress before you go home."

An unmistakable look of relief swept across the young Amish woman's face. "*Denki.* My *mem* and *dat* would ask a lot of questions if I showed up in a wet, dirty dress."

Point made.

Christina gave the girl a quick nod and disappeared

toward the back of the clinic. He heard the unmistakable crank of a noisy knob on a washer and the gush of water filling the tub.

Cheryl put her hand on Naomi's shoulder. "Going to that party was a dumb idea."

Naomi frowned. "I thought I could patch things up with Lloyd."

Dylan wasn't interested in Naomi's love life, but he wondered what this Ben knew about Naomi getting drugged. "Do you know where this Reist boy lives? I'll call the sheriff and have them run by his house. Get a statement."

Naomi looked up with worried eyes. "I'll be ruined if the police are involved. My parents will find out. They won't understand." She pulled the sleeves of the oversized sweatshirt down over her hands. "I should have never gone to that party. My *mem* and *dat* would be disappointed."

Dylan understood all about disappointing a parent. His demanding father wasn't exactly reasonable. And his mother died when he was barely eight. She had been the calming force. The reasonable one.

"Here's the thing…" Christina reemerged from the laundry room, as if she had been giving something considerable thought. "Dylan can help without getting the police involved. Give us the address and we'll check it out."

Naomi shook her head frantically. "I don't remember."

"Cheryl knows, then," Christina said, obviously not taking no for an answer.

Dylan cleared his throat. "You were fortunate nothing more happened." He hoped they weren't making a leap in their assumptions. "We need to find out who may have drugged you."

Naomi's hand flew to her midsection. She looked like she was going to be sick. "I can't get involved." She balled up the cuff of her sleeve and pressed it to her lips. "I don't know the address or anything."

"I don't know the exact address, either, but I know how to find the house. I'd have to show you. There was a sign in front," Cheryl said.

"I want to forget this night. *Please.*" Naomi bowed her head and covered her face with her hands. "I want to forget it ever happened."

Christina pressed the palms of her hands together. "You can't go home until your clothes are cleaned, right?" She opened her eyes wide, pleading. "We'll take a drive in Dylan's truck. You can show us the location. We won't stop. We won't get out of the car. No one will ever know it was you. Okay?"

"Why?" Naomi said, the defeat in her tone evident. "It won't change anything."

Dylan was about to say something when he noticed the rigid set of Christina's body. Anger and maybe something akin to regret flashed in the depths of her eyes. "You'll never forgive yourself if you don't. I know it doesn't seem that way now, but it's important that you seek justice." Christina's voice cracked over the last word and she shook her head briefly, as if trying to snap out of it. "Another young college girl was drugged recently at a party. We need to put a stop to this."

Dread knotted Dylan's gut. Christina spoke as if this were personal. *Was it?* Had something happened to her? Shame washed over him. He had returned to Apple Creek with his own bags packed to their bursting seams with regret, guilt and anger. Never once did he consider that Christina—the physician with wealthy parents, the woman who had everything, the woman who followed her dreams—had had her own share of troubles.

"The Amish ways are not like yours," Naomi said flatly. "We handle things among our own."

Christina blinked her eyes slowly, as if trying to tame her frustration. "I consider you a friend, Naomi. We've chatted a bit each time when you've come in to work, right? I know you're happy in the Amish community."

"Yah."

"This person may try to spike other girls' drinks. He may have already done it."

"Are you serious?" Cheryl asked in disbelief, her long ponytail swinging as her hooded eyes darted from Christina to Dylan and back to Christina.

"Yes, I'm serious." Christina threaded her fingers and held her hands in front of her, pleading with Naomi. "I want you to show us, but I won't force you."

Naomi rubbed her forehead with the cuff of her sleeve, then pulled it away, revealing watery eyes and a tear tracking down her cheek.

"Yah," Naomi whispered, her shoulders easing down from her ears. "We'll show you. But please don't tell anyone."

Cheryl was the far more chatty of the two as she gave Dylan directions to the location of the party. She seemed to enjoy the spotlight. Something about it rubbed Dylan the wrong way, or maybe her manner seemed so forward in contrast to Naomi's quiet nature.

"How did you two meet?" Dylan finally asked.

"Naomi cleans homes in town." Dylan wished Cheryl would let Naomi speak for herself.

"The extra money helps my family," Naomi said, her voice low.

"You were at the Webbs' house—right?—and heard about his party." Cheryl didn't wait for Naomi to answer. "Aaron Webb had a big party and invited you. I was floored when I found out you were Amish." She scooted up on the edge of the backseat so her voice got louder. "Naomi was dressed normally, like in jeans and T-shirt." Then as if realizing her backhanded slam, Cheryl added, "I mean, you weren't dressed Amish. Anyway, we started seeing each other around at different parties and stuff and became friends. Like what, six months ago?"

"Yah." Naomi sounded resigned. "Cleaning all those homes, I started to think I'd rather live in the outside world. But I was wrong."

"Well, thanks." Cheryl laughed, obviously not offended.

"You know what I mean," Naomi said. "I'm more suited to the Amish Way. I went to the party tonight dressed the way I was raised because I was hoping to talk to a friend. I wasn't looking to drink and I certainly never expected to have someone put something in my drink." Her voice grew softer and Dylan looked in the rearview mirror to see Naomi staring out the window. "I should have never had that beer."

Christina shifted in her seat to face Naomi. Christina's hair had begun to dry in ringlets around her face. "None of this is your fault."

"Turn right at the stop sign," Cheryl interjected.

In the rearview mirror, Dylan noticed Naomi biting her bottom lip. Something about this entire story didn't add up, but it wasn't his job to figure it out. He wasn't FBI. Not while he was on leave. He was a college professor. He was only here because he cared for Christina and for the well-being of this young woman.

Dylan stopped at the corner and was surprised to see a young Amish man in a wagon entering the intersection. It was after ten in the evening. The rain had stopped and a bright moon illuminated the countryside.

In the back, Naomi gasped and slouched in the seat.

"It's Lloyd," Cheryl whispered, a hint of awe in her voice. Then to him and Christina, "Lloyd Burkholder is the boy Naomi hoped to see at the party."

Naomi covered her face with the palm of her hand. It was unlikely the young man would have recognized anyone inside the dark cab of the truck, but she obviously didn't want to take any chances. "He'll never take me back if he thinks I haven't forsaken my former ways. Do you think he knows what happened?"

"You know how people talk," her friend said. "You'll have to explain what happened. He'll take you back. I know it."

"How can I explain when I don't even know?" The young woman sounded on the verge of tears.

"I'll help you any way I can," Christina said. "Maybe you should reconsider calling the sheriff."

"Neh."

The horse and wagon proceeded through the intersection and Lloyd tipped his broad-brimmed hat in their direction, not an unusual gesture in the friendly Amish community.

Dylan lifted a hand in greeting, then turned right as instructed. He knew they were almost near their location when Naomi slid farther down in her seat; any farther and she'd be curled up in a ball on the floor. "The barn is behind the house with the sign on the front lawn."

Dylan scanned the landscape and noticed a gold Sold sticker splashed across an Apple Creek Realty sign staked in the front lawn. The house and adjacent barn were dark.

"Doesn't look like anyone's moved in yet," Christina said, her voice barely above a whisper. "Do either of you know who was hosting the party?"

"Neh," Naomi said.

"A bunch of kids probably heard it was an empty house. Prime party spot," Cheryl said. "I heard about the party in town."

"I don't see any cars or horses by the barn." Dylan slowed to a near stop.

"Like I said..." Cheryl sounded like a girl who didn't like to repeat herself. "Everyone scattered when Ben went tearing out of there with Naomi in the backseat."

Dylan glanced over at Christina who seemed intent on studying the landscape. "Do you think anyone's still out there?" she asked.

"Not likely. Don't you remember bolting from a party when you were a kid? They're probably long gone by now."

Christina clasped her hands in her lap. "I'm not sure what we should do now." She glanced over her shoulder into the backseat. "Are you okay, Naomi?"

"I'm *gut.*"

"Please know you can talk to me anytime. Sometimes after the event..." Christina's voice trailed off and she seemed to change course. "Know that I'm here."

"Yah." Naomi's reply sounded less than convincing. "How did you know Lloyd was supposed to show up?" Naomi asked Cheryl.

"Just heard a bunch of people talking, that's all." A

hint of defensiveness crept into Cheryl's tone. "You were the one who really wanted to go."

"It wonders me what I was thinking." Naomi tugged on the bottom of the sweatshirt. "Lloyd, the boy in the wagon, was courting me. We rode home together after Sunday singings. I thought it was a matter of time before we started making plans for marriage. And then…" She sniffed. "I started to doubt things. I met Cheryl. I thought she had so many more choices in life. I thought maybe it would be fun to live *Englisch*."

"Bubble burst." Cheryl laughed and Dylan watched her make an explosion gesture with her widespread fingers.

Dylan drove past the property, scanning the entire area without detecting anything suspicious lurking among the shadows. But that only meant the kids were good at hiding. He went to the first cross street and turned around.

"When I realized Lloyd wasn't there, I was upset and decided to have a beer." Naomi's voice got very soft. "I'm stupid."

"You're not stupid, Naomi. Don't be hard on yourself." Christina shifted in the seat next to him.

"I had the beer and then I felt dizzy. Tired. I still feel a little dizzy."

Christina sighed. "The lab will be able to determine from your urine sample what they gave you."

"I don't see why it matters. I want to forget the whole thing."

"That's probably a good idea," Cheryl said. "Easier to move on. Lloyd will never know what happened. You guys might get back together yet."

Dylan cut a sideways glance at Christina. She was clenching her jaw, obviously holding back. Staring out the windshield, she asked him in a softer voice, "You see anything suspicious?"

He shook his head. "It's dark. Once they scatter, it might be near impossible to find the responsible party. Especially if Naomi's memory is hazy. And if she doesn't want to pursue this."

"I don't," Naomi spit out, probably the most forceful thing she had said since they got in the car. "What Amish man will want me if he thinks I've been…" She let her words trail off. "Nothing really bad happened to me. Someone put something in my drink. I'm fine now. But I don't want people to talk about me. Make up stories about things that never happened."

Christina turned to face Naomi as best she could. "Don't blame yourself."

"I went to the party. I drank the beer."

"That doesn't give anyone the right to take advantage of you."

"Nothing happened," Cheryl repeated, a hint of annoyance in her tone. "Everyone said Ben noticed you acting strangely so he got you out of there. Ben's a good guy."

Naomi sniffed but didn't say anything.

"Let's go back to the clinic. See about Naomi's dress. Once it's dry, she can change, then I'll drive her home," Christina said with her well-honed bedside manner.

"What will I tell my parents?" a panicked Naomi asked, as if she had only now thought of the fact she'd have to go home eventually. "They'll wonder where I've been. I hadn't planned on staying out this late."

"I'll walk you to the door," Christina said. "If it makes it easier for you, I'll explain that you were with me. They know you clean my office. We'll omit the details so you don't have to lie." Christina paused. "If you think that will help."

"Yah, denki."

When they reached the clinic, Dylan climbed out of the car and met Christina, Cheryl and Naomi at the door.

"Well, I better go," Cheryl said. "I don't imagine Naomi's parents will want me dropping her off."

Naomi smiled, a sad smile that didn't reach her eyes. "Thank you for being a *gut* friend."

"I try," Cheryl said with more than a hint of self-deprecation. "Even though being English is rotten eggs and you'd rather be Amish."

Naomi's eyes widened. "It's not that."

Cheryl smiled and took a step backward toward her car. "I was teasing. Trying to lighten the mood." Then Cheryl's expression grew somber. "I feel bad that I didn't warn you to never leave your drink unattended. They taught us that in high school health class."

"Do you remember who gave you the beer? Was it already opened?" Dylan asked, mentally scolding himself for not asking the question earlier.

Naomi slanted her eyes away as if giving it considerable thought. "I don't remember."

Cristina unlocked the door to the clinic. "I'll go check on her clothes."

They made small talk while they waited for Naomi's clothes to dry. Finally, once they were done, Christina handed them to Naomi who gave her a weary smile.

"Go change and we'll take you home."

Naomi disappeared into the exam room and Dylan turned to Christina. "Chasing down the bad guy goes above and beyond the duties of the town doctor."

Christina's eyes held a clarity he had never noticed

before. "If I don't help her, who will? She'll never go to the police." Turning her back to him, she straightened a stack of papers on the counter behind her. "It will eat at her forever."

Dylan resisted the urge to touch Christina's arm, to comfort her. He could tell by the rigid set of her shoulders that his attempts would only be rebuffed. He wanted to ask her so many questions, but right now, one question lingered foremost on his mind. "What next?"

She turned around. "Take Naomi home."

"That's fine. But you can't go snooping around on your own. It's not safe. Do you think, even if they're kids, that they'll take kindly to you turning them in for using drugs?"

Christina jerked her head back. A shadow lurked in the depths of her eyes. "Snooping around? Don't make it sound like I'm some cartoon sleuth."

Dylan held up his palms, realizing his protective—his controlling—nature had offended her. "I don't want you to get hurt," he said, softening his tone.

"I know. And I appreciate that." She tilted her head. "What brought you out here tonight anyway?"

"I thought you might have changed your mind about that ride, with the rain and all."

"I'm fortunate you were there. Thank you." The corners of her mouth tipped up, softening the concern in her eyes. "But please don't think I'm helpless. I can take care of myself."

"We don't know if this is related to the other assault where the girl was drugged." He widened his eyes, trying to emphasize the seriousness of this situation, trying to dissuade Christina from asking too many questions on her own. "We're talking about a real sociopath." He paused a minute. "Who does that? Who drugs women at parties?" The criminal mind had always fascinated him, especially the moment a person took their first steps toward a life of crime. How did a person go from hanging out, drinking with friends, to drugging drinks? Was it premeditated? Random? Or was Naomi targeted?

Dylan missed working a case for the FBI. Teaching law and ethics didn't give him the same adrenaline rush.

"Promise me you won't go looking for trouble." As soon as the words left his mouth he regretted them.

Christina planted her fists on her hips. "I've run this clinic for years. I've dealt with everything from runny noses to spaced-out patients trying to get me to write them a script for painkillers so they could get their next high." Her eyes flashed anger. "I know how to handle myself. I know how to handle people. I know how to dial 9-1-1. *If* someone thinks he can drug girls at parties, he needs to be stopped." She crossed her arms tightly over her chest. "I have every right to ask questions. And I'm careful. I know it can be a dangerous situation."

Dylan dared to step forward and touch her chin with a hooked index finger. He waited for her to look up at him. When she did, he said emphatically, "Not. Your. Job."

Christina jerked away. Her eyes narrowed into dangerous slits. "No, I suppose it's my job to patch up the women *after* they're attacked."

Christina woke up in the middle of the night with a blinding headache. Fortunately it had dulled to a quiet roar by morning. She was grateful for that. Lying awake most of the night rehashing the events surrounding Naomi had contributed to her blah feelings. But as much as she'd like to, her work ethic wouldn't allow her to stay in bed all day. Before Georgia, she could never call in late. Even now, she didn't like to take advantage. But today she decided she had to. Fortunately, Georgia had already been scheduled at the clinic this morning and insisted she had everything covered.

By the time Christina climbed behind the wheel of her sedan and pulled out onto the main road, the mid-morning sun was like needles to her eyes. She dropped the car's sun visor and grabbed her sunglasses. *Ahhh...*

As Christina drove to the clinic, almost on autopilot, she rehashed, yet again, the events of last night. After Christina and Dylan had dropped Naomi at home, Christina had called her brother, a sheriff's deputy. She hadn't wanted to betray Naomi, so Christina left her name out of the conversation, but she needed to let Nick know that someone had potentially drugged a young Amish woman at a party. Law enforcement often watched trends. Maybe someone would be arrested for a similar incident.

Christina purposely omitted the part about almost getting run over in the parking lot. Her overprotective brother would have lost all perspective then. However, Christina had hoped that when her brother tracked down Ben Reist, he would shed new light on what had transpired last night. And he'd probably reveal Naomi's name, but in good conscience, Christina couldn't let the perpetrator go unchecked. Unfortunately, Nick had called her late last night to say that Ben had not come home.

Christina wasn't sure how to feel about that. Maybe Ben wasn't such a good guy after all.

When Christina reached the stop sign at the same intersection they had come upon last night, she found herself turning toward the barn where Naomi had most likely been drugged. She hoped that maybe she would see something in the daylight that she had missed in the dark. The thought of letting the person who drugged Naomi get away with it galled her.

You let someone get away with it. The familiar, mocking voice threaded its way through her brain, not helping her headache. Not one bit.

This is not about me, her rational voice countered. *This is about Naomi.*

Determined not to let her doubts pull her off course, Naomi drove toward the barn then wondered if she had gotten turned around. She wasn't exactly the queen of directions. A car with an attached trailer sat in the driveway. It wasn't until Christina drove past that she saw the unmistakable Sold sign and the barn behind it.

Her pulse raced in her ears and her mouth went dry.

Ignoring all the alarm bells in her head, Christina slowed to a near crawl. The front door was propped open, as if movers were bringing in boxes. Her heart raced as she heard Dylan's stern warning not to do any investigating on her own. Then anger seeped in to replace her anxiousness. What right did he have to tell her what to do?

What harm could it do to knock on the door and welcome new neighbors to the small town? People still did that right? *She* had never done it, but people did. Indecision had her shifting her foot from the brake to the accelerator.

Go to work.

Go. Go. Go.

No. No. No.

Before she had a chance to overthink it, she glanced in the side mirror, the rearview mirror and over her shoulder, then made a sharp U-turn. She slowed and turned into the driveway and parked next to the trailer and climbed out.

As she approached the house, she promised herself she wouldn't go inside, instead staying out in the bright sunlight. *What could happen out here?* She knew better, but she couldn't stop herself. Naomi's sweet face flashed in her mind. She had to do this for Naomi.

Christina hadn't yet figured out exactly what she'd say when a frail woman appeared in the doorway, her head wrapped in colorful fabric. The woman came up short, surprise evident on her pale face. She hadn't been expecting anyone.

"I'm sorry. I didn't mean to startle you." Christina smiled, suddenly feeling foolish.

The woman's skin seemed translucent. Dark shadows marred the skin under her eyes. The vibrancy of her blue eyes wasn't diminished by the lack of lashes or brows. The pretty scarf hid what was no doubt a bald head. A hesitant smile graced the woman's thin lips. "May I help you?"

Christina blinked rapidly. Not planning ahead hadn't been a good idea. It was so unlike her. She had always planned ahead. College. Med School. Clinic in Apple Creek.

Check. Check. Check.

Yet here she was, gesturing awkwardly toward her car, partially hidden by the trailer. "I was driving by the house and noticed someone was moving in. I thought I'd stop by and welcome you to Apple Creek." She really wished she had thought to stop by the diner to pick up one of Flo's pies or something. Well, truth be told, she hadn't expected to see cars in the driveway or to stop when she had.

"Thank you." The woman's reply came out more like a question.

"My name's Christina Jennings. I'm a physician at the healthcare clinic in town."

The woman nodded slowly, as if she was still trying to figure out what this woman was doing in her front yard. "Any relation to Nick Jennings?"

"Yes." Christina smiled. "He's my brother."

"Small town, right? I knew him from way back when. Actually my husband knew him. My name's Linda, by the way."

Before Christina had a chance to ask her more questions, Linda descended the steps and crossed over to the trailer. The back doors were yawning open. The woman reached in and slid a box toward the edge of the trailer and stopped. "I'm sorry, but I don't have time to chat. I have a lot of work to do."

Christina glanced toward the house, wondering if this woman was alone. "Can I help?"

The woman blinked slowly. "No, thank you." She leaned her hip on the back of the trailer, as if the short walk had drained her. "I'm sorry. I don't mean to be rude. I'm tired and there's so much to do. My son and his father are supposed to help me, but apparently there's some work to be done on the mechanicals in the basement." She lifted a thin shoulder. "Figures the first thing we realized this morning was there was no hot water." She frowned. "We had some work done on the house for the past few months. Then we moved a lot of the big stuff in last week, but we had cleaning and the rest of the packing to finish before we could completely move in. It's been a long road, but we're almost there…" She drew in a deep breath, then exhaled. "And I'm tired." She shook her head and gave a weary smile. "Wow, didn't mean to unload on a complete stranger."

Compassion warmed Christina's heart. "Moving is a lot of work. I moved not long ago myself." She remembered the cleaning and the sorting and the lifting, and she had been healthy. Christina couldn't imagine the strain on top of a serious illness.

"Had you moved away from Apple Creek?"

"Oh, no, I just recently relocated a little farther out into the country. I like the space." Christina didn't mention that she grew up in the large house on the escarpment. Her parents' sprawling estate was a landmark of sorts in town, an oddity. However, depending on how well Linda knew her brother, she might already know all that. "How about you? What brings you to Apple Creek?"

A shaky hand went to the woman's head covering. "My son, Matty, and I lived only ten minutes away. We were in a rental. His father—" there was something about the way she said "his father" and not "my husband" that was very telling, or maybe Christina was reading too much into it "—recently got a job in Apple Creek." She held out her palm. "So here we are. Looks like we'll be here for a while."

"I hope you enjoy your new home." Christina shrugged off a vague sense that she used to know this woman.

Linda looked around, as if tuning into her surroundings for the first time. "All this space…this far out in the country. It'll take some getting used to." Her words had a wistful tone. "It seems so remote."

Christina found her opening. "Well, there's another reason I stopped by."

"Oh?" Worry lines creased Linda's eyes.

"Was anyone in your barn last night?"

"No." Her answer seemed too abrupt. "Why do you ask?"

"Oh, it's just…well…" Christina stammered. She *never* stammered. Her comment to Dylan last night that she wasn't some cartoon-character sleuth was about to come back to haunt her. That's exactly how she was acting. Unprepared. Foolish. Babbling. "I was driving by here and I thought I saw some activity by the barn."

Linda frowned. "I'm not aware of anything, but I didn't stay here. We arrived this morning."

"Did your husband or son stay here?"

She hesitated for a moment and the color heightened in her cheeks. "No, we were too busy packing for the big move." Linda stifled a yawn. "The move is wearing me out. I really need to get back to work." Her tone reflected her frustration and embarrassment heated Christina's cheeks. She was usually socially aware, but she didn't want to leave so easily. She wanted to find out more about the barn party held here last night.

Linda pulled the box from the edge of the truck and its weight seemed to pull on her arms. "I better take this in. Nice meeting you."

Christina wrapped her arms around the edge of the box, taking the brunt of the weight. "Please let me do that."

"Thank you." She released her grip on the box. "I need to learn how to accept help. I'm not as strong as I once was."

"You're welcome." Perhaps God had placed Christina here for this one small kindness today, to help her get out of her own head and her own problems.

Linda hurried ahead of Christina, leading the way. Christina was grateful the box wasn't that heavy. Once they stepped into the foyer, Linda pointed to another box. "Please, put it next to that one." The smells of fresh paint and new carpeting permeated the air.

Christina pressed her lips into a thin line and nodded. She placed the box on top of another one. She didn't envy the work ahead of this woman. "If you need anything, please feel free to contact me. I'm only a few minutes away in town. At the healthcare clinic, as I mentioned before."

Linda waved her hand in dismissal, then her eyes brightened. "Thank you." She lifted her fingers to the scarf wrapped around her head.

"If you need help with any of this…" Christina held her hand out to the boxes scattered around the foyer.

Linda shook her head. "There's two able-bodied men who live here. *They* can get after these boxes."

Christina laughed. "Well, I do run the clinic. So, if you need anything in that regard…"

"I'm getting the best possible treatment at Roswell Park in Buffalo. It's a bit of a drive…but…"

"Oh, yes, Roswell is well respected. I guess I meant if you needed anything and didn't want to drive all the way into Buffalo." Christina was careful about how she worded things.

Deep voices could be heard floating up through the vents from the basement. Christina glanced around the cozy house that was still in need of a little TLC, but would surely make a comfortable home. She brushed at the dust on her pants. "Nice to meet you, Linda. Can I bring in a few more boxes before I go?"

Linda shook her head vigorously. "Oh, no… I've already imposed too much. Thank you for stopping by. I appreciate your introducing yourself to me." The poor woman had probably thought a local gossip had alerted the town doctor that a woman with cancer had moved in, when that was not the case at all.

However, would the truth be any better? That Christina had stopped by to see if the occupants had held an underage drinking party on their property? But it seemed—like Cheryl had said—some teenagers had taken advantage of an empty house to party. More than likely, they wouldn't be back now that the house was occupied.

"If you see anyone out back, perhaps hanging around your barn, can you call me?"

"Um…sure." Linda took the business card with Christina's contact information on it and turned it over in her hands. An unease rolled off Linda's thin frame. "Do you think that's something I need to be worried about?"

"It was probably teenagers." Christina feared she had already said too much. She cleared her throat and rubbed her hands together. "I should go. Please call if you see anything…or if you need anything."

"Who are you talking to?" A gruff male voice sounded from the back of the house, sending goose bumps racing across Christina's skin.

Linda held out her arm and began to usher Christina toward the door. "Thanks again, Christina. I'll definitely contact you if I need anything."

Christina stepped outside, the door still propped open.

"Aren't you going to introduce me to your visitor?" The man's voice got closer. Christina spun around and froze in her tracks.

He had more lines at the corners of his eyes and less hair on his head, but he had the same darkness in his eyes and smug look on his thin lips.

Roger Everett. Her brother Nick's good friend. A captain in the army. That's how Linda knew her brother. Christina thought she had looked familiar, but her illness had made her gaunt.

Roger Everett. The name of the man she'd never forget.

The man who had attacked her several years ago.

The man she had been too afraid to accuse.

And now he was here, back in Apple Creek.

THREE

"Christina? Christina Jennings? Is that you?" Roger Everett's lips curved into a smarmy grin—could only she see that?—yet his tone was that of a long-lost friend. Christina felt all the blood drain from her face and she sent up a silent prayer that she wouldn't pass out right there.

Roger lifted his arms as if to embrace her and Christina held up her hands to block him. "Roger Everett." The two words spilled out of her mouth. The smile plastered on her face—a smile for his wife's benefit—hid the icy terror pumping through her veins.

"You remember Nick's sister?" Linda asked, curiosity in her large eyes. "I don't recall having met her before. When did you meet her?"

"Of course I met little Christina Jennings. Oh, wait, she's Dr. Christina Jennings now."

Linda squinted at her. "I don't…"

"I'm not sure we ever met. Maybe only in passing," Christina stammered.

"How is Nick?" Roger asked, carrying on this cheery charade.

"Good." Christina's heart was nearly rioting out of

her chest, but she had to keep her cool. She'd had a lot of practice playing it cool under fire. She was a physician, after all. "You haven't seen him lately?"

"Ah, ya know. Now and again. Everyone's so busy, especially now that he has a little one. How is the baby?"

"Fine." Christina didn't want to give this man any more information about her family than necessary. She cleared her throat. "I didn't mean to intrude. I saw the trailer…" Christina stared at him as the walls in the foyer swayed.

Since Christina had refused to accuse Roger of wrongdoing soon after he attacked her, she wasn't about to start now. His wife was ill. Christina didn't want to cause her any more stress. "I was…on my way out." She stepped onto the porch and backed down the steps, holding the railing. She spun around and walked briskly toward her car.

"What brought you out here?" Roger called after her.

"I didn't know who bought this house. I wanted to welcome the new family to the neighborhood." She aimed her key fob at the car and the locks chirped. She struggled to stay composed as a familiar fear crawled up her spine and stiffened her back.

"Christina mentioned someone was using our barn for an underage party last night," Linda said.

Anticipation made Christina's skin tingle. A few feet from her car, she stopped and turned around. "I'm not sure of the exact location," she backtracked, suddenly feeling like she had betrayed Naomi. The idea that Naomi was drugged on the property of the same man who had attacked Christina swelled like a tsunami in her brain, ready to sweep her under. The coincidence was too great.

"Why would you think that?" Roger asked, a hint of accusation in his tone.

"I may be mistaken." Christina hated the indecisiveness in her tone. *Leave. Just leave.*

"Let's be sure now. Let's take a look. If there was a party, they probably left behind garbage. Beer cans, stuff like that, right?" Roger stepped off the porch and approached her. "Since you took the time to stop, it'd be a shame if we didn't investigate. Or maybe we should call your brother, the deputy." Roger had a way of speaking that was overtly condescending.

"I really should go. I'm running late." Christina's stomach sloshed with dread. She was back in college, trying to escape Roger's grabby hands.

"No, no. I insist. I don't want anyone using my property for parties." He shook his head as if it were truly a great hardship. "Can you imagine the liability if someone got hurt on my property? Or after they left because they had been drinking? I don't know if the bank has cashed the check on the first premium on my homeowner's insurance." Roger held out his hand, encouraging Christina to walk in front of him. The only reason Christina moved was because she didn't want him to touch her.

Not again.

Christina glanced over her shoulder at Linda, willing her to walk with them. The last thing she wanted to do was go to the back of the property into a darkened barn with a man who had forced himself on her when she was in college and then accused her of not knowing what she really wanted.

Never mind that he had a son and a wife at home. Then. And now. Strange that Christina had never met

Linda face-to-face until now. Roger probably had preferred it that way. Easier to lure unsuspecting women.

Nausea roiled in her stomach.

Once they were halfway across the yard and it was clear that Linda wasn't going to follow them, Christina stopped, never turning her back to Roger. She didn't trust him.

She should never have trusted him.

And she was done being polite. Especially when it came to her safety.

She pointed her finger at him. "I can't believe you have the nerve to show your face in Apple Creek."

Roger pressed his hand to his chest in a "who-me?" gesture and his expression took on an offended air. "Nerve?" He leaned close and she did her best not to show her fear. "Your guilt has gotten the best of you. You wanted me, but then your conscience couldn't deal with the fact I had a wife and child." His eyes twinkled with wicked delight. "I'm separated now." He reached out to brush his fingers across her cheek and she backed away.

"Separated from Linda?"

"Yes. Does that make you feel better?"

"Why should it make me feel better? You attacked me." Anger roared in her ears.

"You wanted it," he bit out. "Don't rewrite history."

A steel rod of courage stiffened her back. "I was naive and didn't report the incident. I'm no longer that same girl."

"What is that supposed to mean?" Roger spit out, his face suddenly flushed with rage.

"Someone barely escaped being assaulted on your property and I don't think it's a coincidence. Once a creep, always a creep."

His cheeks puffed and his breath grew ragged. He jabbed his finger in her direction and she struggled not to cower. "You watch out, little lady, or I'll press charges of slander."

Christina glared right back at him. "The truth is a valid defense."

"You got a lot of nerve coming out here…" Spittle flew from his lips.

"I'm done." She gave one last look at the abandoned barn, a row of hay bales with targets on them lined up on one side. She was disappointed she wouldn't be able to investigate further. Not now. Not with Roger. She turned to go back to her car, a surge of adrenaline mingled with dread and anger.

Roger's arm snaked out and grabbed her wrist, and terror pressed on her lungs. Instinctively she yanked her arm, but Roger tightened his grip.

"How do you think the fine residents of Apple Creek would feel if they knew their respected town doctor had tried to break up a marriage? I believe *home wrecker* is the term."

Christina glared at him, then down at his fingers encircling her wrist. Anger made her bolder than she had a right to be. Roger was probably twice her size. "Let. Me. Go."

Roger let go of her wrist and stared at her, daring her to move. "Who do you think the members of this town are going to believe? The war hero who's returned home to take care of his ailing estranged wife despite their differences? The former all-star high school baseball player? The newest member of the town council? Or the town doctor who grew up in a life of privilege—entitlement—and never knew the meaning of the word *no*?"

"No one who knows me would characterize me like that."

Roger hiked a shoulder. "Want to try them? And tell me, why didn't you tell your brother about us?"

"There was no us." She gritted out the words.

"Okay, why didn't you tell him I supposedly attacked you?"

"You know why." She wasn't able to hide the black eye from her brother so she lied and said her roommate had accidentally elbowed her in the eye. Nick felt guilty that he hadn't walked her home from the party that night. He'd never forgive himself if he knew it was his friend who had attacked her. His friend who would have done far more to her if she hadn't fought so fiercely. If something hadn't spooked Roger. She never did figure out what that was.

More importantly, Christina couldn't risk Roger seeking retribution from Nick during a time of war. Roger was her brother's superior in the army. If Christina's accusations fell on deaf ears, she'd risk putting her brother's life in jeopardy while they were serving overseas together. And Roger seemed exactly like the kind of person who might try to get even.

She couldn't risk telling anyone.

A voice roared inside her. *How is your silence any different from Naomi refusing to call the sheriff? It's all a matter of self-preservation.*

Self-preservation and protecting those she cared about. She was afraid of Roger, but she was more afraid of how her accusations back then would have affected those around her. Around her brother.

And a little voice in her head always prompted one nagging question: Had she asked for it? Had she been partially responsible for his assault on her? Christina had been enjoying the harmless, flirtatious banter with her brother's good friend, until it ceased to be flirtatious or harmless.

She thanked God every day that she had been able to escape with only a black eye, and bruised ribs and thighs from his clawing at her.

Her injuries—the assault—could have been far worse.

"I suggest you don't cause trouble for me now," Roger said, his eyes sparking with anger.

Squaring her shoulders, Christina took a step closer. "I may have kept my mouth shut back when you attacked me. I was young. Naive. But I plan to do whatever it takes to protect the young women in town."

A line marred his forehead. "Let me get this straight. You think I'm attacking young women from town?" He jabbed his finger in the direction of his barn. "In my own barn?" He shook his head and leaned in closer; his coffee breath assaulted her nose. "You really are whacked."

His words struck like a punch to the solar plexus and she struggled to fill her lungs with air. He had used similar words to intimidate her into silence years ago, calling her accusations ridiculous.

Roger gave her a curious stare. "I'm a respected member of the town council now. I took over the seat vacated when Old Man Siegfried kicked the bucket. I put some feelers out there when Linda asked me to come back home. She's not doing well," he added, with the first hint of humanity. "I need to be here for her and my son. We don't need your harassment."

She fisted her hands. Was he making a play for her sympathy? She wasn't buying it.

"Why stir up trouble from so long ago? It'll be my

word against yours. A ruined reputation is tough to re-build."

"Stay away from me." Her voice came out low and threatening.

"You stopped by my house," Roger reminded her.

"My mistake." She turned toward her car. She couldn't bear to spend one more minute with this man.

"Keep your mouth shut, Christina. Linda doesn't need your false accusations. Her health can't take it."

"That's on you. Not me." Christina kept walking and Roger followed close behind.

"Let me make this clear and in terms you'll under-stand. If you stir up trouble, you'll be sorry."

"Is that a threat?" All her nerve endings hummed and she fought to hold it together. "You're good at threats."

"People love war heroes," he said, his voice strangely even.

Christina lifted a shaky hand to her forehead. "I should never have stopped here." She started jogging toward her car parked in the driveway.

"I thought you wanted to check the barn," Roger hol-lered after her.

Christina didn't answer, nor did she stop until she was locked inside her vehicle and had started up the engine. She was about to press her forehead to the steering wheel when a shadow crossed her lap. She glanced up to see a mini-me version of Roger Everett.

Christina opened the window. Before she had a chance to say anything, the young man—who *had* to be Roger's son—said, "My mom and dad are trying to work things out." He stared at her with a steely gaze.

"Okay…"

"If you're one of his girlfriends, you better not come around here anymore." His tone was flat, threatening.

"I'm not dating your father." Her body involuntarily shuddered. She angled her head to look up at him and she had to shield her eyes from the sun. "How old are you?"

The boy squared his shoulders. "Seventeen."

"Do you know about a party in the barn last night?"

The boy crossed his arms and shook his head. "How would I? We didn't move in until this morning."

"Okay," she said, noncommittally. She didn't want to call him out. Maybe he had innocently mentioned to some kids at school that he had a vacant house. It wouldn't take a bunch of kids long to figure out it was a prime location for an unsupervised party.

"I better go." She put the gear into reverse, then looked up at him. "I'm a physician in town. If your mom needs anything, here's my card. I gave your mom one, too. Feel free to call if you have concerns. It can be hard to care for someone who's sick."

Half his mouth quirked into a wry grin. "My mom's going to be fine." Reluctantly, he took her business card and stared hard at it.

"I'll keep her in my prayers," Christina said softly, not really sure what else to say.

Something flashed across the young man's face, as if he wanted to say something sarcastic, but instead he took a step back and flicked his hand in a farewell gesture, and she thought she heard him mutter, "Thanks."

Dylan drummed his fingers on the steering wheel as he waited in the parking lot of an abandoned restaurant surrounded by cornfields. Ben Reist, the young man, who had unceremoniously dumped Naomi at the clinic door in a driving rain, lived nearby with his mother. Christina had called Dylan, her voice trembling and anxious, determined to find Ben Reist. Now.

Something was wrong.

To be on the safe side, he'd told Christina to meet him in a neutral location and they'd head to the boy's house together. Dylan was grateful his summer classes had yet to start, affording him the opportunity to be there for Christina. However, he didn't understand why she insisted on trying to track Ben down when her brother, the sheriff's deputy couldn't. Dylan had no authorization to investigate this case and Christina most definitely didn't.

"Where are you?" he muttered to himself.

The sound of gravel crunching under tires had him turning to see Christina arriving in a ten-year-old sedan. She parked across from him and climbed out of the car. Her long brown hair was pulled into a ponytail and a concerned expression marred the corners of her mouth. An ache of nostalgia expanded in his chest.

He had been a fool to let her go.

Dylan pushed open his car door and climbed out. "What's going on?"

Christina crossed her arms and glanced toward the street. Something flickered in the depths of her eyes, something he couldn't quite pinpoint. "What's wrong?" he asked when she didn't answer his first question.

She paced in the small space between their parked cars, kicking up gravel. She stopped suddenly and drew in a deep breath, her shoulders rising and falling with the deliberate action. His heart sank at the pained look on her face. He felt like this was one of those moments when his life was going to shift off its tracks. He crossed his arms to brace himself.

She closed her eyes for a moment, then searched his face. She stepped closer and touched his arm. "I have to tell you something and you can't get mad. You can't seek revenge because if it gets out, the repercussions might ruin my career." Her voice cracked.

"What is it?" A sharp blade of fear twisted in his gut.

"I stopped by the house where the party was last night."

"What?" The heat of anger exploded in his head, but he gritted his jaw to keep it in check. He had no right to tell Christina what she could or couldn't do. It wasn't his job to protect her.

It had been his job to look out for his rookie partner. And look what had happened to her.

Inwardly, he shook the thought away. He wondered if he'd ever be able to outrun that nightmare.

"I was going to work and took a quick side trip. I couldn't help myself."

He opened his mouth to say something but stopped when Christina held up her hand.

"There was a trailer parked in the driveway and it was obvious someone was moving in. I stopped and met the new owners. They claim they weren't home last night."

"You mentioned the barn party?"

"Yes, but I kept Naomi's name out of it."

"Did they know anything about it?" Dylan couldn't fault this woman's tenacity, but she shouldn't be putting herself at risk.

"Claimed they didn't know about it."

"Even though I don't agree with your stopping at the house by yourself, you answered the obvious questions. Make sense. Empty house. Empty barn. Prime place to hold a party."

"But there's something more." Christina looked down at the ground and moved the gravel around with the toe of her tennis shoe. She swept a strand of hair away from her face and Dylan thought he detected a tremble in her hand.

"What is it?" He frowned, unease tickling at the back of his throat.

"I know the owner of the house. He's a friend of my brother's." She seemed to flinch at the word *friend*.

Dylan held his breath waiting for her to continue.

Christina lifted her chin and locked eyes with him. "This is where I need you to promise me you won't do anything…"

"How can I make a promise when I don't know what you're talking about?" Cold dread weighed on his chest.

"Roger Everett attacked me shortly before my brother and he were deployed. My brother's first deployment, Roger's second."

"Your brother was deployed a month after we broke up." Another point that made Dylan a complete jerk when it came to cutting off the relationship with Christina. A surge of panic and adrenaline coursed like daggers of ice through his veins. Dylan's vision tunneled and all he could see was Christina's pretty face. "He attacked you?"

Christina pressed her lips together as if she were trying to contain her emotions. Dylan resisted the urge to pull her into his embrace, comfort her.

Her lower lip trembled and she nodded. "A few of us went to the beach along the lake for a send-off party. Roger was always friendly to me, so we stayed and chatted long after most people left." She pressed a hand to her mouth before she continued, "He tried to force himself on me and I had to fight him off."

"Oh, man…" Dylan turned to look away. "I'm sorry."

"Not your fault," she said rather glibly. "I should have known better. Shouldn't have put myself in that position. He had a wife and child. What was I doing flirting with him?" Her tone was even, numb. "We were chatting. He was my brother's friend."

"Did he…?" Dylan struggled to get the question out, afraid of the answer. Sorry he hadn't been there to protect someone he had once loved more than life itself.

She closed her eyes and shook her head. "I fought like crazy and God was looking out for me that night. I was able to ward off his advances but not without getting a black eye and some sore ribs. I ran all the way home."

"I'm sorry," Dylan said again. He really was. But if God had been with her that night, she wouldn't have been attacked. A twinge of guilt tightened his throat.

"Why didn't you tell me?"

"You?" The single word was like another stab to his gut.

"You should have told *someone*. Someone you trusted." His voice cracked and he plowed his hand through his hair.

Christina twisted her lips as if considering how to best explain. "My roommate planted the first seeds of doubt. Would people believe me? The Everett family is well respected in Apple Creek. Roger Senior was the mayor at the time. And what about my brother? He and Roger were in the same army unit. Roger was his captain. Would Roger take it out on my brother? I couldn't risk Roger not watching out for my brother."

"So you stayed quiet."

"So I stayed quiet," Christina repeated. She shook her head abruptly as if to clear away the memory. "My brother noticed my black eye when I saw him off at the airport, but I told him my roommate accidentally elbowed me in the eye. He was pretty preoccupied with his deployment and didn't try to pick apart my story." Christina dragged a piece of hair out of her eyes. "I never told him it was Roger. I had to make sure Roger didn't lash out at my brother. These guys need to look after each other."

"Your brother still doesn't know his *friend*—" the word dripped with anger and sarcasm and disbelief "—attacked you?"

"No."

"Now you don't think it's a coincidence that Naomi was drugged on Roger Everett's property."

"I don't know what to think. But I have an idea. Ben Reist, the boy who drove Naomi to the clinic can tell us if he saw Roger at the party."

"Wouldn't it have been strange to see an adult male at a teen party?"

"Yes, that's why I'm hoping Ben would remember if he saw him. I found a photo of him and my brother on Facebook."

"Don't you think you should take this information directly to your brother?"

"I want to ask Ben myself." She raised her chin in expectation. "Will you go with me?"

"Yes, but not because I think it's a good idea that you involve yourself in this investigation. I'm going with you because I'm afraid you'll go without me."

Christina's knees shook as she climbed out of Dylan's truck in front of the Reists' house. What if Ben had seen Roger at the party? Would she finally be brave enough to come forward? Tell people—tell her brother—what happened? Protect other young women from this predator?

A sick feeling swirled in her gut. Had hiding her attack left other women vulnerable? She crossed her arms in front of her, then dropped them to her sides.

I can do this.

"You okay?" Dylan asked as he met Christina around the front of his truck.

Christina let out a raspy breath. "If I had come forward, Roger wouldn't still be out there hurting girls."

Dylan gently touched her arm. "You were the victim. Don't do this to yourself."

"It's hard not to."

"We also don't know what Roger's been up to. He may not have been involved in drugging Naomi. Let's not get too far ahead of ourselves."

Christina nodded. "My brother came here last night. Ben wasn't around."

"Maybe he's home now."

The sound of a door opening drew their attention to the front of the house and they both grew quiet. A woman stood in the doorway behind the screen door watching them. "May I help you?" she called out to them, suspicion lacing her tone.

"Come on." Dylan urged Christina forward with a hand to the small of her back. When they reached the bottom of the porch steps, he was the first to speak. "Mrs. Reist?"

"Yes?" Her posture suggested she was poised to slam the door in their faces as if they were trying to sell her new windows.

"Hello, I'm Dylan Hunter. This is Dr. Christina Jennings." Christina imagined he missed the authority of whipping out his FBI badge. "Is Ben home?"

The woman frowned. "A sheriff's deputy was out here

last night looking for my son. He's still not here. When I heard the car, I had hoped it was him. I haven't seen him since yesterday afternoon." Her tone shifted from annoyance to worry.

"Is that unusual?"

The woman pushed open the screen door and stepped onto the porch. She flinched as the door slammed closed behind her. Her skepticism was evident in the watchful way she studied Dylan and Christina. "Who did you say you are?"

"I'm Dylan Hunter and this is Christina Jennings."

Mrs. Reist dragged a shaky hand across her forehead. "Why are you looking for my son?"

"We wanted to ask him if he saw someone we know last night," Dylan said.

"Why?" the woman asked, obviously not willing to give them any information.

Christina took a small step forward and placed her hand on the bottom post of the railing. She'd have to approach this woman like one of her pediatric patients unwilling to receive his shots. "A friend of mine wasn't feeling well at a party last night and Ben gave her a ride to the healthcare clinic." She paused for a moment. "I'm a physician there."

The woman jerked her head back. "He did?" She made a noncommittal sound. "Nice to see that some of the things I taught him rubbed off." She paused for a long minute. "He's not in trouble?"

Other than leaving Naomi in a heap on the pavement, then nearly running me over, he's a sweetheart.

Christina forced a smile. "When do you expect him home?"

The woman shrugged. "Your guess is as good as mine.

He has a job at the general store stocking shelves. He's got plans to go to college in the fall. Did you know that? First one in our family to go. He's got a nice scholarship." She rubbed her upper arms, pride evident in her eyes. Then her voice grew quiet. "I hope he's not out doing something that will mess it up."

"As far as we know, he was a Good Samaritan last night. We need to talk to him."

"I can tell him you stopped by?"

"Yes, please. Tell him Dr. Christina Jennings from the healthcare clinic stopped by. He'll know who I am." Or at least who she probably was: the woman he had nearly flattened with his car. But she'd be willing to attribute that to his panic. His fear of someone thinking he had drugged the young Amish woman. His fear of messing up his college scholarship.

A dark thought invaded her mind: What if Ben had drugged her, then got cold feet?

Christina couldn't shake her unease over the fact that Roger Everett owned the property. She wasn't a fan of coincidences of that magnitude.

"Thanks for your time," Dylan said, and led Christina back to his truck.

Once they were inside the privacy of his truck, Christina said, "I can't imagine the stress of being a parent. How does she not know where her son is?" She sighed heavily. "I was hoping he could identify Roger."

"Then what?"

"Then I'd convince Naomi to come forward. Maybe Cheryl could testify, too. She might have seen him at the party. Someone needs to stop this jerk. If he attacked me and drugged Naomi years later, how many other victims have there been in between?

"I'd take the photo to Naomi at her home if I wasn't worried about stirring up more trouble for her. I'll show it to her when she next comes in to clean the office."

"Maybe it's time you let your brother do some investigating. Maybe he can ask Cheryl, too."

Christina clutched her cell phone with the photo of Roger to her chest. "How do I tell my brother his good friend is a creep?"

"He'd want to know."

Would he? "I need to get back to work." She'd deal with that dilemma later.

They drove away from the Reists' home and returned to the parking lot of the abandoned restaurant to retrieve Christina's car. The second Dylan turned into the lot, Christina knew something was wrong. As they got closer to her car, she saw cracks like a million spiderwebs crisscrossing her windshield.

The bottom of her stomach dropped out.

"What in the world?" she muttered. With a trembling hand, she pulled on the door lever and Dylan gently touched her arm.

"Hold on. Stay in the truck." Dylan climbed out, assessing the surroundings. Christina understood why he made a good FBI agent and not for the first time she wondered why he had given up his career—even if only temporarily—to become a professor. Cynically, she figured he had gotten bored with it and needed to mix things up. Like he had with her. Before last night, she had effectively avoided him. Since last night, they'd had bigger concerns than prying into his employment history.

Anxious, Christina couldn't remain in the vehicle. Her legs felt weak as she made her way to her car. The glass had shattered in circles where someone had obviously made contact with a baseball bat or tire iron...something hard enough to shatter all her windows.

Nausea swirled in her gut. She moved as if in slow motion toward the driver's side. Dylan stood, blocking her path, an expression on his face she couldn't quite read.

Didn't want to read.

"What is it?" Christina hated the shaky quality of her voice.

Dylan placed his hand gently on her shoulder. "Come on. We can call the sheriff. Then have your car towed."

"No, I need to see." Christina brushed past him and peered through the hole in the driver's side window. Shards of glass dangled from the hole, waiting for gravity to drop them to the ground.

She blinked a few times, trying to process the scene. Her vision tunneled and tiny dots danced before her eyes. Whoever did this didn't leave a note. Instead, they had left a large knife sticking out of her headrest.

Christina turned around, squaring her shoulders. "Who would do this?"

Had Roger already made good on his promise to make her sorry if she caused trouble?

The look of compassion on Dylan's face weakened her steely resolve. She wasn't used to relying on anyone. "What's going on?" she asked, her voice shaky.

"We're going to find out. And I won't let you out of my sight until we do."

FOUR

Rage coursed through Dylan's veins as he inspected Christina's vehicle. He leaned in closer to examine the handle of the knife to determine if he recognized the make. Little details could tell a lot about a perpetrator. Was he military? Maybe? A Boy Scout? Hopefully not.

This particular knife was nondescript. A knife from any steak set on any kitchen counter in America.

In contrast to the generic knife, the attack was definitely specific, targeted. Personal.

Dylan was glad it didn't take much to convince Christina to call the sheriff's department. But he knew it would be a struggle for her to tell her brother her suspicions about his good friend.

The approaching sound of an engine and tires on pavement had Dylan squinting into the sun. He tented his hand over his eyes and was relieved to see a sheriff's car pull up. He turned around as Christina was slipping her cell phone into her purse.

"Nick was in the area." He could read the hesitation on her face.

Dylan wanted to reassure her that everything was

going to be okay, but really it wasn't his place. He had long ago abdicated that position.

Nick climbed out of the car and gave his sister an embrace. "You okay? What happened here?" Nick pushed his hat back on his head, then gave his sister a curious look.

Christina discreetly swiped at a tear trailing down her cheek and nodded against his chest. An emptiness expanded inside Dylan. He had not been able to provide her comfort.

Nick was the first to speak. "Does this have anything to do with last night?" His question was directed at his sister, but his suspicious glare was firmly intended for Dylan.

Nick was very protective of his little sister and apparently he had a long memory for guys who hurt her. Despite the silent tension brewing between the men, Dylan held out his hand in greeting. "Nick, nice to see you."

Christina stepped back. Nick accepted Dylan's hand in greeting and immediately got to business. "What happened here?"

Christina crossed her arms firmly across her chest. "We decided to check in on the young man from last night, Ben Reist."

Nick held up his hands, exasperated. "And you did this why? I would have followed up."

"I know. I just…" Christina cut Dylan a quick glance. "Ben wasn't home anyway, so it doesn't matter. I had parked here and we drove over there together. When we got back to my car someone had vandalized it." Christina kicked at the small gravel stones in the parking lot.

Nick glanced around the area. "Pretty remote location." He rubbed his jaw. "Maybe bored kids."

"They must have been really bored." Sarcasm dripped from her tone.

"I looked up Ben in the system. He doesn't have a record. Unless today was the day he decided to go off the rails, he doesn't seem like a kid who would do this." Nick slowly walked around the car, inspecting it. When he reached the driver's side and noticed the knife, he looked over at Christina, a pinched expression on his face. "This is personal. Who would have done this?"

Christina cleared her throat. "I don't think it's Ben. I think he was a Good Samaritan who was afraid of getting involved beyond helping Naomi." She stammered a bit. "I—I think maybe…"

Christina met Dylan's gaze and he gave her a subtle nod, encouraging her to continue.

"I think Roger Everett had something to do with this," she finally blurted out.

"What are you talking about?" Nick's brows snapped together.

Unease twisted Dylan's insides. He hated that he hadn't been there for Christina when she needed him most. He couldn't help imagining Christina trying to get away from Roger. Panicked.

Dylan gritted his teeth. He had been so determined to find a better job with the FBI in a big city, forgetting those he hurt along the way. He had stomped on her heart without any consideration in order to follow his dreams.

The pain on Christina's face made him realize he had pursued the wrong dream.

"Hear me out," Christina pleaded. "I know you and Roger go way back, but he's not the man you think he is."

"Go way back?" Nick's voice rose in disbelief. "Sarah and I were going to ask him to be the baby's godfather."

He took a step back, seeming to be standing on the edge of control. "Tell me what's going on."

Nick's law enforcement mask slipped firmly into place, hiding the strain evident on his face only moments before.

"Do you remember when I had a black eye before you were deployed, back when I was still in college?"

Pain flashed across Nick's face. "You said your roommate elbowed you in the eye."

"My roommate didn't elbow me in the eye." Christina paused long enough to let it sink in. Dylan felt like he was the witness to something he shouldn't have been privy to. Taking a risk, he lifted his hand and placed it on the small of Christina's back. Her stiff posture seemed to ease.

"Roger hurt you?" Nick's voice shook.

Christina's shoulders rose and fell. "We were the last two at the beach bonfire. The send-off party for you guys." Her voice was oddly calm.

Guilt pinged Dylan's insides. He should have protected Christina. Yet, he realized his guilt was irrational, misplaced. Christina was too independent, too strong willed to have allowed him to be her protector.

Yet the truth was, if he hadn't dumped her, he would have been there that night. Roger wouldn't have had the chance to hurt her.

"Did he...?" Nick's voice cracked as he crossed his arms over his chest and widened his stance, as if being tough could shield him from the pain of his friend's betrayal.

Christina shook her head. "I was able to fight him off." A distant look descended into her eyes. "I'm not sure how, but I did. I escaped with a black eye and a few bruised ribs." She pressed her hand to her mouth, then dropped her hand as if she were reliving the moment.

Dylan was beginning to understand the wall he had sensed around Christina. She had immersed herself in work to avoid getting hurt. If she didn't put herself—physically or emotionally—out there, she wouldn't get hurt.

And could he blame her?

Nick took a few steps toward his sheriff's cruiser, then pivoted back toward them. "I'm going to kill him."

Christina put her hand on her brother's forearm. "Stop. That's not who you are."

"Why didn't you tell me?" Even without seeing it on his face, Dylan could hear the anguish in Nick's voice.

Christina shrugged. "Where do I begin? Maybe it was my fault."

"You can't believe that…"

"You guys were being deployed together. I didn't want my foolish decision to stay on the beach alone with him to jeopardize your safety. I didn't want Roger to take it out on you if I accused him. And I had no proof…" The words poured out of her mouth, as if she had been waiting to reveal her long-kept secret. "And he had a wife and child. I didn't want them to suffer."

Nick pulled his sister into a fierce hug. "I'm sorry. I'm sorry this happened. I'm sorry you couldn't come to me."

Nick lifted his eyes to Dylan, an unspoken truce between the two men. Apparently Nick realized everyone made mistakes.

Nick released his sister, then took off his hat and plowed his hand through his hair. He pointed his thumb at her damaged car. "How does all this tie into last night?"

"Well, my patient—" Christina was careful not to betray Naomi's confidence "—was possibly drugged at a party on Roger's property. I took a urine sample, so we'll see." Christina seemed to be studying her brother's face. "A little too coincidental, right?"

"You think Roger's responsible?" Anger, disbelief, disappointment threaded through Nick's strained voice.

"I wanted to see if the young man who brought my patient to the clinic recognized Roger's photo. A guy our age would stand out at an underage drinking party, either way, but I thought the photo would cement it."

"Why would you do this on your own?" Nick planted his hands on his duty belt.

"I wasn't alone." Christina tipped her head toward Dylan.

"You let her do this?" Nick clenched his jaw, obviously checking his emotions.

Dylan's eyebrows shot up, but before he could say anything, Christina tilted her head and laughed, a sound void of humor. "No one *lets* me do anything. You of all people should know that."

Nick held up his hands in an apologetic gesture. "I didn't mean… I'm worried about you." His brow wrinkled. "You think Roger trashed your car?"

Christina fisted her hands in frustration. "Someone doesn't want me pursuing what happened to my patient."

"How would they know your car was parked here?" Nick asked.

Christina shrugged. "Maybe they followed me?"

"This stops here. Now." Nick turned on his heel to walk away and Christina grabbed his arm, stopping him.

"Wait. We have to come up with a plan," Christina said.

"A plan?" Her brother sounded skeptical.

"Yes. I don't think you should confront Roger."

Nick rubbed a hand roughly across his jaw. "Um… he hurt you."

"Wait. Listen to me. His wife is sick." Christina planted the palm of her hand on her forehead, as if she were racked with indecision.

"Don't you think I know that? He's my friend!"

"Then you'll understand that Linda can't handle any more stress. Of course, I don't want any more women to be hurt, either, but I'm also afraid. What if Roger didn't have anything to do with the incident last night and I'm creating havoc in his life? Well, I'm not worried about his life, but his family's. His wife's. His son's."

"I should forget about this? After what he did to you?" Nick asked.

"Can you investigate without letting on? Maybe Roger'll mess up if he doesn't realize he's a suspect," Christina suggested.

Nick stared at her for a long moment, neither agreeing nor disagreeing. "I'll have your car towed and we'll see if we can get prints." He turned his attention to Dylan. "You'll look out for my sister." It was an order, not a question.

Christina shook her head, a playful expression easing the hard lines around her mouth as if finally revealing the truth had somehow set her free. She planted a kiss on her brother's cheek. "I can look out for myself."

Christina stole one last glance at her poor car as they pulled out of the parking lot. The vandalism was the work of someone who had serious rage issues. Someone who wanted to take it out on her car.

Take it out on her.

No matter how much she tried, she couldn't believe that this was a random incident and that made her feel even worse. Afraid.

She tugged on her seat belt to prevent it from locking across her chest. She felt claustrophobic as it was. "I'm not sure I did the right thing telling my brother about Roger."

Across the cab of the truck, Dylan shot her a glance with a curious expression before turning his attention back to the road. "You've been holding this secret inside for years. You needed to tell your brother."

"What if I've built up the incident to be more than it was?" A shudder rolled through her. A headache started behind her eyes.

Why had doubt taken root now that she had told her brother the truth? It was the truth, right? She hadn't exaggerated the attack in her mind, had she?

Dear Lord, help me navigate these uncharted waters.

"You did the right thing." Dylan spoke with a confidence she could only dream of.

"What if attacking me was a one-off and Roger had nothing to do with the attack on Naomi?"

"Stop *what if*-ing everything to death." There was something in his tone that made her pause.

Christina tugged again on her seat belt as it tightened across her midsection. She really needed air. Food. Something.

As if reading her mind, Dylan said, "Let's stop at the diner and get something to eat. You look a little shaky."

A nervous laugh bubbled from her lips. "Just what a girl wants to hear."

"You know that's not what I meant. I just…" He let his words trail off. "You need to take care of yourself."

"Ha." That's what her mother had always told her: *You work too hard.* Christina wasn't exactly sure what her mother knew about taking it easy. Her parents had been entrepreneurs and world travelers for Christina's entire life.

Then a realization slammed into Christina. "Poor Georgia. I've left her at the clinic all day. I texted her before I left for Ben's, but I never thought I'd be gone this long. I haven't been thinking straight." She dug her cell phone out of her purse and called the clinic. Georgia answered on the second ring.

"All quiet," Georgia assured Christina. "I can handle things. Why don't you take the day off?"

"Day off?" Christina laughed as if the notion was ridiculous. "I'll be—"

Dylan reached over and raised his voice to be heard over the phone. "A day off is a great idea."

Christina playfully punched his shoulder and gave him a pointed glare, but she couldn't maintain her feigned annoyance. She smiled in response to his smile. The smell of his aftershave tickled her nose. "Are you sure, Georgia?"

"I'd be honored if you trusted me enough to run the clinic on my own."

"I do." And that was the truth. Georgia had only worked there for a short time, but Christina had grown to rely on the young physician assistant. As the supervising physician, Christina would review the files of any patients, but there was no reason she had to be in the office. "Thank you. See you in the morning. And please call me if you need anything."

"Sounds good."

Christina ended the call and tossed the phone back into her purse. "I guess I'm free for dinner."

"Does the diner sound good?"

Christina's stomach growled. "Only if it includes apple pie."

"With a side of ice cream."

"À la mode?"

"That's what you fancy people call it. Just give me a couple scoops of vanilla on the side." He laughed, but kept his focus on the road ahead of him. Oh, she had missed that laugh. Inwardly she shook her head. She would allow herself to share a meal with this man, but nothing else. She refused to risk her heart.

Dylan held the door of the Apple Creek Diner open for Christina, but before she went in, the general store across the street caught her eye. Butterflies flitted in her stomach and her mouth went dry.

"Do you think your pie and ice cream can wait a few minutes?" Christina asked, tilting her chin toward Apple Creek General Store. She hoped using humor would ease her growing panic.

"You want to see if Ben's working?"

"You read my mind."

His smile lit up his face. "I wish it was always this easy."

She tipped her head, not wanting to get sidetracked. "Maybe Ben can finally tell us if he saw Roger at the party last night."

"You're not going to let your brother investigate?"

"Let my brother investigate. I want to talk to Ben for a minute. That's all." She bowed her head. "I can't help but think my silence put other women in jeopardy."

"That's a big leap. Even if Ben did see Roger last night, it doesn't mean Roger did anything wrong. He owns the property. He'd have an excuse for being there." Dylan let the door of the diner close and they remained outside.

Christina shook her head in disbelief. "If Ben does recognize him, it wouldn't make sense for Roger not to have admitted to me this morning that he was there." Christina lowered her voice to a hushed whisper, glancing across the street. She figured a person never knew who was listening. "It would have been safer. He could have claimed he was breaking up a party. It would have made sense. But he acted surprised that there was a party on his property at all."

Dylan touched her arm. "Sure, let's go to the general store."

Christina ran a hand across her forehead, hoping to smooth the headache that was pulsing behind her eyes. "I know. It doesn't make sense." She tucked her hands under her arms and rolled up on the balls of her feet. "Really, I can't see Roger smashing my car, because it would only cause more problems for him." Her stomach dropped and her headache grew. "I don't know."

"Come on, before you drive yourself crazy."

They walked across the street. Before they got to the store, Dylan came up behind her. "Hold on."

Christina turned around. "What?" She tried to hide her apprehension behind her curt reply.

"We have to be cautious on how we approach this."

"Help me out then. You're the FBI agent."

She thought she noticed him blanch. "I'm on leave."

"You never told me why that was." She imagined he had gotten bored. Like he had with her.

"You never asked."

She studied him, unable to read his expression. "You're right. But I suppose you'll have to share that story with me another time."

"Fair enough."

Christina pulled open the door and the bells clacking against the glass jangled her brain.

An Amish man in a wide-brimmed hat sat behind the counter, watching them with bored disinterest. "Can I help you?" The man's words had the familiar Pennsylvania Dutch accent.

"Is Ben working today?"

"Ben Reist? *Yah,* he came in. He's in the back."

"What time did he start his shift?"

The Amish man gave her a curious glance from under the brim of his hat. "And you are?"

"I'm Dr. Christina Jennings." She took a chance on the truth. In her heart she felt Ben had gotten himself caught up in a bad situation, but she had to find out if he had seen Roger Everett in the barn before Naomi was potentially drugged.

A crash sounded from the back room. Christina moved toward it, but the Amish man held up his hand. "Hold on. We don't allow customers back there."

Christina's heartbeat raced and she spun around and pleaded silently with Dylan. He grabbed her hand. "Come on."

Dylan hustled out the door, and she had to run to keep up. "Where are you going? Ben's in the back."

"Ben's running out the back door."

"Oh!" Christina pulled her hand out of Dylan's. "Run! Go, don't let me slow you down."

Dylan gave her a sideways glance before she hollered

at him to "Go, go, go." He'd get farther if she wasn't holding him back. She wasn't much of a runner.

She watched as Dylan slipped between the buildings, down a narrow alley. She inched toward the alley, but the dark shadows made her pause.

She hated that she had become afraid again. Feet rooted in place, she waited on the front walk listening for the sound of running or shouting.

Anything.

The silence unnerved her.

Then, the clip-clop-clip of a horse's hooves drew her attention. An elderly gentleman and his wife coasted past in a buggy. The Amish man tipped his hat toward her.

The door on the general store swung open and the bells clattered against the glass. The Amish clerk came through the door holding Ben firmly by the arm. Christina widened her eyes in surprise. "I thought you ran out the back."

The Amish man tipped his head toward the alley. "Apparently so did your friend. But Ben tripped over a few boxes on his way out." He stared at him pointedly. "You are going to have to *red up the room*."

Ben nodded, a look of apology on his face. The clerk let go of the young man's arm and watched him as if he were a puppy in training and likely to dart into a busy intersection. "You wanted to talk to him? Then talk. Make it fast, he has a mess to clean up."

Christina glanced toward the alley, wondering when Dylan would realize Ben hadn't made his escape out the back door. Her mind raced with all the things she wanted to ask the boy. But not in front of his employer. She didn't believe in causing Ben any unnecessary issues. She had heard from more than one source that he had plans for college this fall. Just because her parents had footed the bill for her education didn't mean she wasn't sympathetic to those who worked hard to earn scholarships and money to do it on their own.

After the silence had stretched another unbearable minute, Dylan appeared, his chest heaving from the exertion. He shook his head slowly in disbelief when he noticed Ben standing on the sidewalk.

"We need to talk to you now," Dylan said with the authority of an FBI agent. He turned to the clerk. "We'll send him in when we're done."

The man tipped his hat and shrugged before going back inside the store. Christina figured that was the most excitement the Amish man had probably seen in a long time.

Dylan was the first to speak. "You realize you almost ran over Dr. Jennings last night in the parking lot of the clinic?"

Ben bent his head and toed the crack in the cement with his black sneaker. He finally lifted his head, the first sign of fear crossing his eyes. "I'm sorry. I didn't mean it. I panicked."

"Why?"

"Naomi. Is she okay?" Ben's eyes flashed bright, scanning the street behind them.

"I can't discuss a patient," Christina said with a calmer voice than she actually felt. "But don't worry," she added, feeling compassionate.

"Why did you bolt?" Dylan asked, his tone far more stern than hers. "Why didn't you stay and make sure she was okay?"

"I didn't want to get in trouble. I…" Ben seemed to be studying Dylan, trying to figure out the role he played in this mess… "I saw the truck approaching. I figured it was the doctor. The sign on the door said the doctor would be back shortly." He turned to Christina. "I didn't see you. I'm sorry. I was trying to get out of there before someone blamed me for Naomi's condition."

Then Ben's face grew hard and he squared his shoulders. In a flash, he turned into a belligerent teenager. "Why do I have to tell you?"

Dylan stepped forward. Too bad he had given up his FBI badge, because Christina had no doubt he'd made an imposing agent.

Why had he walked away? Twenty-four hours ago, she'd claimed she didn't care what had brought him to Apple Creek. Told herself she had no reason to care.

Now her curiosity was growing. What had really brought him here?

"You want to play it that way?" Dylan pulled his cell phone out of his back pocket. "Let's give Deputy Jennings a call. He'd be interested to know you tried to run down his sister."

Ben's hands flew up in a defensive gesture and immediately he seemed contrite again. "No, please."

"Tell us what's going on," Christina said, using a coaxing tone.

Ben leaned back and planted the sole of his sneaker on the brick storefront. He hung his head and muttered something unintelligible.

"Speak up," Dylan said, obviously losing patience.

Ben's head snapped up. "I'm not sticking around Apple Creek. I have plans to go to college in Buffalo this fall." His foot slammed down on the sidewalk and he pushed away from the wall. "I was picked up last month for underage drinking. I got it dismissed in court as long as I don't get in trouble again for the next twelve months." He lifted his shoulders to his ears. Suddenly he looked much younger than his seventeen or eighteen years. "I shouldn't have gone to that stupid party."

"You took a chance by bringing Naomi to the clinic. You didn't have to do that." Christina felt like she and Dylan were playing good cop, bad cop. She came naturally to the role of good cop.

Ben nodded. "My sister is friends with the girl who was attacked in the apartment off Main Street. My sister knows I'm going away to college and she told me to look out for my friends." His lips flattened into a thin line. "I was looking out for Naomi. We used to hang out a bit. She was pretty cool for an Amish girl. I was kinda surprised she was at the party. I heard she was making plans to be baptized." He rubbed his forehead. "It was strange she showed up in her Amish clothes. Usually, she'd wear jeans and a T-shirt." He shrugged.

"How did you know Naomi?"

"Through Cheryl. She's in my grade." Ben ran a hand over his short hair. "It's not unusual for us townies to have Amish friends. It's a small town. Some of those Amish teenagers are more wild than my other friends. I think they're getting it out of their system before they get baptized."

"Perhaps," Christina said, unwilling to comment one way or another. She had seen a lot in her years in Apple Creek, too. People were people. Good and bad.

Ben looked up with wary eyes. "My windshield wipers are brutal. I really should get new ones. I didn't see you in the parking lot until the last minute. Honest. I'm sorry."

Christina nodded. "I'm fine."

Dylan muttered something under his breath.

Christina ignored Dylan. "You did the right thing by bringing Naomi to the clinic."

Ben dragged a hand across his mouth. "She's okay?"

"You'll have to reach out to her, but—" Christina smiled "—you did the right thing. Just be more cautious when you're behind the wheel."

"Get new wipers," Dylan added. "And if you ever do something like that again—and I hope you don't—don't drive off. Stop and deal with the situation. That advice will serve you well in life."

Ben swallowed hard and nodded. "I will, sir. I'm really sorry."

Ben tipped his head toward the door of the general store. "Can I go back to work? I don't want to lose this job. I need the money for college."

"One more thing." Christina dug into her purse and pulled out her smartphone. She opened a social media app and entered Roger Everett's name. A few more clicks and she had his image on the screen. With a shaky hand, she held the phone up to Ben. "Do you recognize this man?"

Ben scrunched up his face. "Maybe he's been in the store?" The statement came out more as a question.

"Did you see him at the party?"

Ben pointed at the screen and his face contorted into a look of disbelief. "That dude? He's, like, old."

A man in his thirties wasn't exactly old.

"The party was a bunch of kids. Teenagers. Maybe a few guys in their twenties." Ben shook his head. "But not him."

"Okay." Christina looked over at Dylan. The expression on his face was unreadable.

"If you think of anything else, call me at this number."

Dylan scribbled his number on the back of his FBI card and handed it to him.

Ben did a double take and chewed on his thumbnail. "I'm not in trouble, am I?"

Christina reached out and touched his arm. "When you go to college, keep looking out for your friends, okay? And treat women with respect."

"Yeah, yeah, I will." Ben flicked a glance in Dylan's direction before slipping back into the store.

Christina turned to Dylan, not knowing what to think. "Was I too easy on him?"

Dylan smiled. "No. I think he's a good kid who happens to be a bad driver. If it hadn't been for him, Naomi may have ended up in a far worse position."

Christina's stomach pitched.

How many times had she thought of how *she* could have been hurt much worse when Roger attacked her?

FIVE

Over the next few days, Dylan and Christina got into an easy routine. He picked her up at home, dropped her off at the clinic and picked her up again at the end of the night. Some nights they ate together at the diner, other nights Christina begged off, claiming she was tired. He never knew which Christina he was going to get, but he'd take whatever she was willing to offer. Spending time with her had gotten him out of his head. Out of the nightmare that haunted his restless sleep.

Their conversations never ventured into the personal, mostly circling around the weather, his upcoming classes and the lack of leads on who may have drugged Naomi.

Mostly polite conversation.

It was midafternoon, and Dylan decided to head toward his apartment, dropping off some pie for his landlady, Mrs. Greene. He had a little time before he picked up Christina. A part of him hoped she never replaced her car, because the more time Dylan spent with Christina, the more time he wanted to spend with her. It made him feel like he did back during his college days. Full of hope. Fearless. Excited.

But the events of the past nine months had knocked

the wind out of his sails. He'd come to Apple Creek to get his head on straight. And his connections with the university helped land him a job here.

The sleepy little town had never been his dream. He had always wanted to be an FBI agent in a big city. Once he cleared his head—*if* he cleared his head—he hoped he'd be able to go back.

He'd have to be careful not to hurt Christina, but he'd enjoy each moment while he could.

Dylan reached his apartment in a neat house on the edge of town. Mrs. Greene was sitting on the screened-in porch drinking tea.

Her voice floated out. "I thought this was your break between college terms. You're gone more now than when you were teaching a full slate of classes."

"Ah, well…" Dylan said noncommittally.

Mrs. Greene stood and pushed open the screen door. "Come have some tea with me." As if anticipating his refusal, she waved her hands and didn't meet his eyes. "You won't deny an old lady, now, will you?"

Dylan smiled to himself. He lifted the plastic bag in his hand. "I brought us some pie. Flo made peach."

Mrs. Greene's eyes shone brightly at her good fortune. "I suppose it's a good thing I made fresh tea, then, isn't it?"

A few minutes later, they were sitting at the porch's corner table enjoying iced tea and peach pie. The stress from the last few days rolled off him. "This tastes like the tea my grandma made. She also added fresh lemons and—" Dylan wrinkled his nose. "What else is in here?"

Mrs. Greene smiled brightly. "I'm not telling."

"That's what my grandma used to say."

"We have to hold on to some of our secrets. Otherwise you young folk might decide we're taking up oxygen."

Dylan laughed. Mrs. Greene had a way of telling it like it was.

And Dylan knew all about secrets. His grandmother was the only one who'd shown him compassion and love. His father had ruled with an iron fist and his mother died far too young. In stronger moments, he'd tell his dad he was going to be an FBI agent because he thought it sounded tough. Brave. An FBI agent wouldn't be afraid of anyone, especially not his own dad.

As a young boy, Dylan had had no one to stick up for him except for his maternal grandmother.

"Maybe *your* grandmother will share her secret recipe."

Dylan smiled woefully. "Grandma died when I was twelve." At that point he'd realized he was alone in this world. For a long time Dylan filled the loneliness with school and then his career in the Bureau.

That was, until Nora was gunned down.

His father's mocking words—" Yeah, you'll make a great agent"—scraped across his brain. Then he'd throw back his head and laugh, the silver fillings of his teeth visible in his gaping mouth. The grating sound still rang in his ears. Turns out his father had had the last laugh, after all.

In the end, Dylan Hunter hadn't been the successful FBI agent he'd thought he'd be. He failed himself. He failed his partner.

"I'm sorry to hear that," Mrs. Greene said, snapping him out of his reverie, "I'm sure your grandmother would have been very proud of you, a professor." Mrs. Greene gave him a satisfied smile. "It's a noble career."

She cocked her head, studying him. "But, if you ask me, you don't look much like a professor type." Mrs. Greene had always been so forthcoming, he was surprised she hadn't told him this before.

"I was an FBI agent before I traded my badge for a tweed coat." He respected that, although chatty, Mrs. Greene never pried more than he allowed her to.

"Ha! I've never seen you wear a tweed coat."

Dylan ran his finger across his chin. "I've been meaning to get one." They both laughed.

"FBI, huh?" Mrs. Greene seemed to size him up. She pointed at him. "Now, that makes sense."

He laughed.

"You look more like law enforcement than a professor." She leaned in conspiratorially. "You must be bored to tears here in Apple Creek. Oh." Her eyes lit up. "Are you here undercover? My sons are in law enforcement. You guys are all adrenaline junkies."

"I don't know about that…" His mind flashed back to the night when, nauseous with fear, he found Nora's lifeless body in the doorway of one of their confidential informants'. She had gone to see the junkie on Dylan's instructions. The guy had been generally harmless and Dylan suspected his partner might have been able to get the snitch to talk more. She had a way with people.

Instead, Dylan had gotten his rookie partner killed.

How had he misread the situation? How had he not known the informant was dangerous? From that point on, Dylan had made one reckless move after another and had to step away from the Bureau when he almost got himself shot on a collaborative drug raid with the DEA. Right then and there, still with his flak jacket on, he knew he had to take a break. Clear his head before any more blood was on his hands.

"Something bad happened. Made you want to get away." Mrs. Greene smiled sadly.

"I needed a change."

"But you miss the work."

Dylan scooped up the remaining crumbs on his plate with his fork. "No, can't say I do." The words rang false in his ears.

"Ah, well, didn't mean to pry." She sounded skeptical. Mrs. Greene's gaze turned toward the street.

A sheriff's cruiser pulled up in front. Dylan slid his chair back from the table when he noticed Nick climb out and push his hat up on his forehead. "I better see what the deputy wants."

"How do you know he's here for you?" Mrs. Greene asked, curiosity lacing her tone.

"Is there any reason the deputy would be here looking for *you*?" Dylan widened his eyes and smiled.

Mrs. Greene lifted her head to study Deputy Nick Jennings. "Sadly, no."

Dylan shook his head and laughed. "Excuse me a minute."

He met Nick on the sidewalk and nodded in greeting. "Do you have any news on the barn party?"

Nick shook his head. "I've been quietly keeping an eye on Roger. Don't want to raise any red flags until we have some real evidence." He sounded like a man who had been severely disappointed. That happened when your sister told you your good friend had attacked her.

Dylan held up his palms. "Why did you stop by?"

"I appreciate your looking out for Christina. Between

my shifts at work and the new baby at home, I'm not able to check in on my little sister like I'd like to."

"No problem. Summer session doesn't start for a bit yet. I've got nothing but time." Dylan smiled despite the hum of unease that stretched between the two men.

"The thing is…" The deputy took off his hat and dragged a hand over his head. "Maybe it wasn't fair of me…"

"No, really, I don't mind."

"When I said it wasn't fair, I wasn't referring to you." Nick shot him a sideways glance. "I was referring to my sister."

Dylan jerked his head back. "Someone has to keep an eye on her."

Nick ran a hand across his chin, giving it some thought. "You do realize she'd lay into both of us if she heard us talking about her like this?"

Dylan laughed, feeling some of the tension easing away.

"My head tells me my sister is more than capable of standing on her own two feet. She always has been. My parents raised three independent kids. But I don't want you to hurt her."

"I don't plan on it," Dylan said, bowing his head. The dappled sun, filtering through the spring foliage, danced on the sidewalk at his feet.

"You really did a number on her years ago."

"That was never my intention." The half-truth slipped from his lips. *What had he intended?* Perhaps he had never intended to fall for the pretty young coed in the first place.

The tension crackled in the air. The two men stood as if ready to draw guns in a duel.

"If you hurt her, I will find you," Nick muttered.

"Good to know."

Nick gave Dylan a curt nod. He waved to Mrs. Greene, then climbed into his cruiser and drove away.

Dylan's phone rang in his pocket. He pulled it out, not paying attention to the number.

"Hello."

"Dylan, it's Christina. I hate to bother you—" The shaky quality of Christina's voice kept him on edge.

"No, no problem. What is it? Need me to pick you up?"

"Cheryl, Naomi's friend, stopped at the clinic. I'm worried about Naomi. Can you come down here? Now?"

Christina sensed Dylan standing in the hallway near the back of the clinic before he said a word. She looked up and smiled briefly, relief washing over her. Funny how she had come to count on him in such a short time. His presence felt familiar. Comfortable.

"Hold up a minute." She made a few notes about her last patient on the digital tablet in front of her, then set it aside. "Thanks for coming here early. I didn't mean to sound the alarm."

"No problem. What's up?"

Christina looked into Dylan's warm brown eyes and he genuinely seemed to mean it. He seemed more compassionate, less…tough…than he had when she had dated him years ago.

Less to prove.

As a young college student, she had fallen for his take-charge attitude, but it was that exact personality trait that had driven him to leave her behind to pursue his FBI career. He'd still never shared why he had taken a detour into academia, but part of her was afraid to ask. Afraid to learn it was only temporary and that he'd be leaving Apple Creek soon.

Christina held up her index finger. "Let me check the waiting room." She hustled to the front and found the lobby empty, then came back to find Dylan sitting on the edge of her desk behind the counter.

"What's going on? I thought you said Cheryl was here."

"She was, but she was anxious to leave. I figured there was no point making her stay. She said what she had to say."

"Which was?" Dylan crossed his arms over his dark blue golf shirt. It was a nice color on him. She quickly dismissed the thought.

"Cheryl said she and Naomi had a falling out. She said Naomi wouldn't talk about the other night—"

"That's normal, right?" Dylan interjected.

"It can be. But Cheryl said they'd been friends for a while and Naomi was acting strangely. Wouldn't tell her what it was about. Cheryl thinks she's hiding something."

"I don't understand. Isn't it normal for Cheryl and Naomi to drift apart? Cheryl's not Amish and Naomi is. I can't imagine what they'd have in common, especially if Naomi was committed to being baptized."

A twinge of guilt gnawed at Christina. Perhaps she had shared too much about Naomi's life with Dylan over their shared meals. She let her shoulders drop and leaned back, resting her backside on the lower counter across from Dylan. "Cheryl said that Naomi might not be telling the whole truth about the other night at the barn. About the drugs. When I suggested Naomi might not remember things clearly because of the drugs, Cheryl said it was more than that. That Naomi was being particularly evasive."

"About what?" The intensity rolling off Dylan unnerved her.

"Cheryl thinks Naomi may have gotten the drugs from the clinic." Christina lifted a shaky hand to her forehead; the news had rocked her to the core. She had trusted Naomi.

She still trusted her. It was only a rumor.

"Do you think she's capable of stealing drugs?"

Christina's hand instinctively went to the keys in her pocket. "We keep the drug cabinet locked." She bit her lower lip. "I've had no reason to suspect Naomi of any wrongdoing, but...it wouldn't be impossible for her to access the drugs. She cleans for me. Maybe if I left it open during a busy moment. Or Georgia...or if Naomi swiped the keys at a moment of inattention." A band of unease tightened around her lungs, making her dizzy. "It's all possible."

Christina worked her lower lip. "The lab got back to me. An antianxiety drug was in Naomi's system. I checked our medicine log. I'm missing meds." She bit her bottom lip. "It doesn't mean she took them. But I don't know..." She pulled her shoulders up to her ears, then let them drop.

"We'll figure it out," Dylan assured her.

"Cheryl's suggesting Naomi stole the drugs, then took them to the barn party and took too many. Naomi was rushed here unconscious, so it's possible, but why would Cheryl tell on her good friend *now*? It seems too convenient." She ran a hand down her long ponytail. "Or maybe she's genuinely concerned about her friend's welfare."

Christina glanced down the hallway to make sure no

one had slipped in the front door. She didn't want anyone to overhear their conversation.

"Cheryl claims she's worried about her. That maybe she'll do something drastic with the drugs because she doesn't seem happy."

"Is there a reason she's not happy?"

Christina measured her words carefully. She didn't want to betray Naomi, but she also needed Dylan's help to reach her. "Cheryl told me Naomi might be pregnant."

Dylan slumped back, his mouth widening in surprise, as if Christina had shown up on his porch with a bouquet of balloons and an oversized check for a million dollars.

"Wow!" he said, "I thought the Amish were conservative."

"Generally, but teens are teens. They're not always thinking about the consequences of their actions."

"And Cheryl thinks Naomi might hurt herself because she's in a desperate situation?"

"Yes." Christina scratched her forehead. "More desperate than most teens because she's Amish. And Cheryl doesn't know who the father is. Naomi was tight-lipped about that."

"And Cheryl wants you to reach out to her?"

"Yes. Naomi doesn't want her parents to know she's still associated with the townies, so Cheryl doesn't think she should go. But if I go to the Mullets' farm, it might not seem unusual because Naomi works for me."

Dylan pushed off the edge of the desk and stood in front of Christina. His eyes moved around the space as if trying to process what she had told him.

"Now you're thinking maybe Naomi took the drugs on her own and you opened an old wound by telling your brother how Roger attacked you."

Christina bowed her head. "Amazing how well you know me."

Dylan hooked his finger under her chin and forced her to look at him. "Regardless of how Naomi was drugged, Roger did attack you. That hasn't changed."

"But maybe—"

"No maybes. It was long past time you talked about the attack. You did nothing wrong."

Christina slipped out from behind the counter, feeling hemmed in. "I honestly don't know where to go with all this. We have Naomi, who was drugged at a party, and then while we're trying to find answers, my car is vandalized. I was convinced Roger was trying to threaten me into silence. Maybe bored kids damaged my car. Maybe there are no connections. Maybe I just have a black cloud hanging over my head."

"There are a lot of unanswered questions. I still think you need to be careful."

"I will." She paced the small space between the counter and one of the exam rooms. "Would you come out to the Mullets' to talk to Naomi with me? We need to get her side of the story." She lowered her voice. "And if she's pregnant, she'll need support and prenatal care."

"Of course."

"Let me lock the front door." Christina dropped her white coat off her shoulders as she walked down the narrow hallway. She drew up short when she noticed Linda Everett, Roger's wife, sitting in the otherwise empty waiting room.

"Mrs. Everett." Christina's feet felt rooted in the worn carpet. A flush washed over her. Had Linda overheard their conversation? She swallowed hard. "How can I help you?"

A tired smile curved the woman's pale lips. The dark marks under her eyes had grown a deeper shade of purple since Christina had first met her.

"You stopped by the other day and told me if I ever needed anything…" Linda's voice was hoarse.

"Of course, of course." Christina flipped her jacket back up on her shoulders and held her hand out. "Come back. What can I do for you?"

Had Roger told his wife about Christina's accusations? Of course not. She wouldn't come here if he had.

Christina directed Linda to an empty room and told Dylan she'd be a few minutes. She closed the door and expected Linda's expression to change to one of anger or rage or maybe denial. But all she saw was fear and exhaustion. Maybe this was just a regular visit.

"How can I help you?"

"I have wonderful doctors in Buffalo, but lately I feel like I'm dragging Roger or my sweet son Matt to Buffalo for them to adjust my pain meds. A long, exhausting trip. And Matt hasn't had his driver's license that long. And Roger's so busy with his new job." She shook her head, as if these thoughts had been keeping her awake at night.

"Is there something I can do for you?"

"Maybe you can consult with my doctors. Maybe I won't have to go all the way to Buffalo for adjustments to my pain medication."

"You're uncomfortable?"

The woman furrowed her brows as though to ask if there was any doubt.

Christina understood that the end was approaching. Her heart broke for Linda. And her teenage son.

Not that long ago, Christina had cared for her brother's mother-in-law during the end stages of cancer. Nick's mother-in-law had lived a long time with a relatively high quality of life under Christina's care. Christina had grown more spiritual as she assisted Mrs. Gardner during her last months of life.

But it had also taken a toll. Made Christina realize how fragile life was. How quickly someone's world could turn upside down.

The reality of life's fragility made Christina immerse herself even more completely in work. The most control she felt in her life was when she was busy. Helping patients.

Christina turned to Linda, knowing she was in a precarious position, considering she was married to the man who had given Christina nightmares. "I can help you. Whatever you need."

Linda blinked slowly and a single tear tracked down her cheek. Christina wondered if she owed this woman the truth about her husband. But something made her keep her mouth shut. Linda was already suffering. Knowing her husband was a jerk—if she didn't already know it—would do nothing for her overall well-being.

Linda dragged her oversized purse onto her lap and fumbled through it. She finally pulled out a business card and handed it to Christina. "This is my doctor in Buffalo."

Christina took the card and glanced at the name. "I'll contact Dr. Meckler's office and see what they're giving you. Maybe I can catch him now."

Linda's shoulders sagged in relief, the sharp angles of her frame visible under her shirt. "Thank you."

"Hold on a minute while I make the call." Christina slipped out of the room.

Dylan stood there with his car keys in hand. "Everything okay?"

"Yes." Their gazes lingered for a minute.

"I'll be in the car. Give you some privacy. Take your time."

"Thanks." Christina smiled her appreciation. She dialed Linda's physician's office and sent up a silent prayer when his office staff connected her rather quickly with the doctor, who had been in his office doing paperwork at the end of the day. They discussed Linda's treatment and the best options for pain management. Christina hung up and prescribed a stronger pain medication. She called the script in to the Apple Creek Pharmacy.

Christina went back into the exam room and shared the information with Linda who thanked her and stood to leave. Linda's clothes hung off her thin frame. "Can I call someone for you?" The thought of Roger coming by the clinic to pick up his wife sent Christina's mood spiraling.

"I should be fine to drive home. I can drive short distances."

An unmistakable urgency surged through Christina. She cleared her throat. "Have you had any other issues with kids using the barn for parties?"

Linda paused for a minute and a tinge of pink colored her cheeks. "Not at all," she said a little too emphatically, or maybe Christina was reading too much into it.

"That's good." Christina traced the edge of the tablet where she entered all her medical files. Then she lifted her eyes to meet Linda's. Something compelled her to keep pressing. "I need to ask you another question. Has Roger ever hurt you?"

Linda's eyes flared wide. "Why would you say such a thing? He has never hurt me." She glanced down at the carpet and then touched the bandana neatly wrapped around her head. "We had our differences over the years, but mostly because the war made him a tougher man. But he is here now. When it counts." She lifted a shaky hand to her mouth, then quickly dropped it. "He's here for me. More importantly, he's here for Matt. Our son is going to need his father now more than ever. So, no, he hasn't hurt me. And whatever you think he did to you, you're wrong. He has been nothing but a friend to you and your brother."

Christina took a step back and nearly stumbled backward. "He...he told you?"

"Of course he told me. He figured you were the type to cause trouble."

"When did he tell you this? Years ago or just recently?"

Linda jerked her head back. "Only recently. He had no reason to say anything sooner. You're making this all up. And to do so now is just unconscionable."

The hot fingers of regret tightened around her neck. Christina wanted to argue, plead her case, but decided Linda's well-being was more important. "I didn't mean to upset you." She waved her hand, wishing she had kept Roger's name out of their conversation. "I'm not looking to cause trouble for your husband." Christina hesitated a fraction. "If you thought that was the case, why are you here?"

Linda blinked slowly and flinched. "I don't have the time or energy for drama. I've heard you're a good doctor. And I'm in pain. I'm desperate."

Christina nodded, feeling like she had been scolded. She paused briefly and gathered her thoughts. "I sent a script for pain meds to the local pharmacy. I hope our conversation won't stop you from coming here if you need something. Anything."

Linda nodded almost imperceptibly. Christina had a tough time reading her.

"Cancer sucks, ya know," Linda muttered.

"I do."

Christina witnessed the depth of Linda's pain and in that fleeting moment, Christina decided she had to let it go. She would not destroy what little peace Linda had these last days on Earth.

This woman was battling for her life. What point would it serve if Christina insisted on making Linda see who her husband really was?

A whisper of doubt haunted Christina.

What if Naomi had fabricated the events of the other night to cover her drug use?

What if Christina had been the only one Roger attacked?

What if Christina *had* been the only one to blame?

When Christina emerged from the clinic a few minutes after the patient left, Dylan climbed out of his truck to greet her. If he hadn't, he would have felt like one of those guys who honked for his date in the driveway, something he'd never do.

"Everything okay?" he asked, watching her expression closely. Christina used to wear her emotions on her sleeve, but now, all these years later, she was much more stoic. Reserved.

Time and life experiences tended to do that to a person. For him, life had made him more compassionate. More leery. Whereas Christina had seemed to don a suit of armor.

Maybe it was an act. A means of self-preservation. He understood that. Self-preservation had landed him in Apple Creek.

"The patient who just came in. That was Roger's wife."

Dylan jerked his head back and bumped his elbow on his open truck door. "I shouldn't have left."

Christina lifted her hands and a flash of something he couldn't quite name—anger, defiance, frustration maybe—flashed in her eyes. She stopped in front of his truck and crossed her arms, her body posture unmistakable. "Do you think she was going to hurt me? Come after me for accusing her husband of attacking me? Did you notice how frail she was?"

"Why are you so angry?" He shrugged. "Was it something I said?"

"I've managed fine for years without you. Don't think you have to be my protector now that you've decided to come back around."

Dylan held up his hand and clenched his jaw. "Hey, hey, what's going on?" He reached out to sweep a strand of hair off her face and she batted his hand away.

"Stop."

He dropped his hand. "Why are you angry with me? Someone vandalized your car. They impaled the headrest with a steak knife. Don't I have a right to be concerned?"

"You lost that right when you dumped me."

Dylan voice grew soft. "What happened in there?"

Christina spun around, marched to her side of the truck and climbed in.

Dylan got behind the wheel but didn't start the engine. He could sense Christina cooling off.

"I'm sorry," she finally said. "I have no idea where all that came from. I'm stressed. I'm wondering if I'm a good judge of character at all. This has nothing to do with you. With us. I'm mad. That poor woman is in the fight of her life and her husband is a jerk. How much can one person endure? I'm mad that Cheryl planted the idea that Naomi stole drugs from the clinic. I'm mad that I may have unnecessarily stirred up things with Roger at a time when his wife needs him most."

"It's not your fault that Roger is a jerk. Do criminals get a pass because someone in their family is sick?"

"No," she said curtly. "But I kept my mouth shut this long, it wouldn't have killed me to keep it shut a little while longer." She shook her head and slumped into the seat. She reached back, grabbed the seat belt and snapped it into place. "I jumped to so many conclusions the minute I discovered Naomi had been drugged on his property." She tugged on the belt across her lap.

Dylan leaned close to her and smiled, but she refused to look at him. This woman had such a tender heart. "You are helping her. You're not causing anyone any anxiety."

The hint of a smile tugged at the corners of her mouth. "Except for you." A full smile split her lips, revealing perfectly straight, white teeth.

He brushed his knuckles across her smooth cheek. "Just a little."

Christina shrugged and leaned toward the window, breaking the spell. She pointed at the ignition. "Start the truck. We need to talk to Naomi."

SIX

"Park on the road." Christina leaned forward, watching three young Amish girls holding hands and turning in circles. A tune reached her ears, one that sounded like "Ring Around the Rosie," but not quite. Naomi was standing near the girls with her back to the road.

"I'd like to talk to Naomi alone. Do you mind waiting here?"

Dylan smiled and it struck her in this moment that she'd forgotten how truly handsome he was. "No problem." He powered both windows down then leaned back in his seat, getting comfortable.

"I won't take long. I think she's more likely to talk to me alone."

"Go on, then."

Christina climbed out of the truck, feeling a little guilty that she was all Jekyll and Hyde with Dylan. She couldn't make sense of her own feelings and she wasn't about to let the walls down to let him in. Too many people in her life had walked away or had always been at a distance, including her parents. They were loving when they were around. They were generous, but they had never truly been present in her life. Or the lives of her two siblings.

She loved her parents for all they did. For all the opportunities they provided for her and the clinic. But she had often wished they had been like other parents. Present at the sidelines when she decided to try high school volleyball or there to drive her to dance class before she realized she was uncoordinated. But without her parents, she'd never have been able to open and run the clinic. And for that she was forever grateful.

Not to mention they paid her medical school tuition.

The breeze cooled Christina's cheeks and snapped her back to the moment. She crossed the yard, trying to shove aside the feelings and nostalgia, and wondering how she was going to broach this topic.

Did she believe Naomi was capable of stealing drugs from the clinic? It didn't seem possible. But it wouldn't be the first time a friend had betrayed her trust.

A niggling unease sent a pall over the gorgeous spring day.

When Christina was halfway across the yard, Naomi turned around and noticed her. Her pale skin was nearly the color of her white bonnet. She didn't look well. Naomi's attention flitted from the barn, to the house, then back to Christina. Naomi held up her hand to the young girls and said something in Pennsylvania Dutch that Christina didn't understand. For all her years in Apple Creek, she only understood bits and pieces of their language.

"What are you doing here?" Naomi asked, pink splotches blooming on her pale cheeks.

"It's okay." Christina kept her voice low. "I don't want to cause any problems with your family."

Naomi bowed her bonneted head. "Why are you here then?" She lowered her voice. "Did Cheryl send you?" She glanced furtively toward the barn. "Never mind. My brother Paul is nearby. Please leave. He can't know about any of this. Besides, I have to go in soon to help my *mem* with the evening meal. "

One of the little girls chased a volleyball in their direction. Naomi kicked it away and the girl skipped squealing after it. "If someone asks, tell them I stopped by to give you your work schedule and pay you." She reached into her pocket and handed her an envelope. "Your pay."

"I normally pick that up."

"Not today." Christina smiled, trying to make Naomi feel at ease, to get her to open up. Christina always fancied she had a good bedside manner, but dealing with the Amish required a certain amount of diplomacy.

"Your friend Cheryl is worried about you," Christina whispered.

"What did Cheryl say?" There was a cynical note to her voice.

Christina resisted the urge to put her hand on the young woman's arm. "She's worried…" She let the words trail off, figuring the less she said, the better.

"I—I—" Naomi stuttered.

The three little Amish girls laughed and giggled about twenty feet away. The dichotomy of the tableau hit Christina. The little sisters were safely ensconced in their insular way of life while their big sister was standing on a precipice between the only life she'd ever known and the big world out there.

Christina was worried the young woman had made some bad choices that would forever change her life.

Something about Naomi's situation resonated with

Christina but she couldn't quite grasp its significance, like a shadow scurrying past a window out of the corner of her eye.

"I met a boy when I was cleaning the Webbs' house."

Christina held her breath, waiting for Naomi to continue.

"Aaron Webb. He's twenty and I thought…" She shook her head. "I thought he loved me."

Christina's chest began to tingle as she anticipated the conversation to come. The one she had heard many times from young girls who had come into her clinic, panic stricken that they had made an impulsive decision. One that changed their lives.

Naomi was flirting with the temptations of the outside world. With grown-up situations. Christina wanted to pull the girl into an embrace and assure her everything would be alright.

But she didn't know that it would be alright.

Christina flicked a glance toward the truck where Dylan was patiently waiting. He seemed to be looking at something in his hand, most likely his phone.

Christina turned her back to Dylan, to the little girls playing in the yard. She leaned toward Naomi. "Are you pregnant?"

Naomi's lower lip trembled and a single tear tracked down her cheek.

"We can run a test at the clinic. If you are, you need to make sure you take care of yourself."

Christina lowered her eyes and said a prayer for Naomi. If she had found herself involved with an English boy and was now pregnant, her life was going to be forever changed.

"I don't know. I told Cheryl I was worried."

A need to counsel this young woman overwhelmed Christina. Her question about the drugs would have to wait. As she formulated a plan in her mind to help, a young man stormed out of the barn, rage flashing in his eyes. *Naomi's brother*. Christina reflexively stepped back, fearing he was coming at her, but instead he stopped inches away from Naomi.

"You are bringing shame to this family." He shook his gloved hand. "You're breaking *Mem's* heart."

"Paul, please. Stop." Naomi's voice shook.

Naomi's brother stood there with barely contained rage simmering below the surface. Naomi turned to Christina. "I have work to do. Thank you for dropping off my pay." Naomi made a show of holding up the envelope.

Naomi ushered Christina away from her brother. "When do I work next?" Naomi asked, louder than necessary.

Christina whispered, "I can help you."

Naomi glanced back at the barn and presumably her brother, but she still took the time to lean in and whisper frantically in Christina's ear. "As you know, I went to the party the other night because I thought Lloyd Burkholder was going to be there."

Naomi smoothed out the folds of her dress. "Lloyd took me home a few times after Sunday singing. That was, until I got too worldly. I was foolish to think that was my world. Then, I thought maybe I could convince him to take me back. Marry me. Pretend the baby was his. That's why I went to the party. That's all. I wasn't dressed *Englisch*. For the first time in a long time, I wasn't trying to pretend I was something I'm not."

Christina glanced toward the barn to make sure Naomi's

brother wasn't listening. "There were drugs in your system after the party."

Naomi's eyes grew wide with worry. "Will they hurt my baby if...?" She couldn't even say the words.

"You'll need to get proper prenatal care." Christina drew in a deep breath, then asked the question that was on her mind. "Did you take the drugs from the clinic?" Even as she asked the question, she knew the answer. Naomi wouldn't have knowingly taken something—never mind *steal* something—that could jeopardize the health of a potential pregnancy. And why would she have submitted to a drug test? It didn't make sense. Someone had drugged her.

Naomi clutched her apron and looked like she was going to pass out. "I would never, Dr. Christina. Never."

"Okay, okay, I believe you."

"I only went to the party to try to win Lloyd back. If he married me, I could spare my parents the shame of having an unwed mother for a daughter."

"Does your brother know?" Christina thought of Paul's angry outburst.

"*Neh, neh.* He'd run to my parents. It wonders me that he hasn't already because he knows I've been hanging out with *Englisch* friends. Paul has never diverted from our Amish upbringing. He's *gut.*" Naomi tugged on the strings of her bonnet, her anxiety evident on her face.

"Naomi, you can't keep running away from your problems. You need to come to the clinic. Soon. Take a test." Christina purposely omitted the word pregnancy.

Naomi pressed her lips together and stared at Christina, unwilling to acknowledge the horrible predicament she was in. She swiped at a tear rolling down her cheek.

"Naomi!" Paul shouted.

"You need to go." Naomi gently nudged Christina toward the road, then she raised her voice solely for her brother's benefit. "Thank you for bringing me my pay."

"I didn't mean to interrupt your day." Christina attempted to smooth things over. "Good night."

The little Amish girls went back to their game, holding hands and running in circles, their sweet voices threading through the tension in the air. So innocent.

Their sweet, sweet innocence.

The smell of stale air rushed at Christina when she opened the door to her sealed-up home. Between work and chasing demons, she hadn't spent much time there lately. She needed to open the windows. Do some spring cleaning. Air out after the long winter.

Christina tossed her purse on the couch and was struck by how much she loved her house. She had been excited when she found this cute little place not too far from the center of town, but not too close, either. It afforded her the privacy she needed.

The one-story house with a wide porch was a far cry from the palatial estate where she had grown up. When she was a little girl, she'd envied her friends who seemed to have moms waiting for them with warm cookies when they got off the bus in front of homes like the one she lived in now.

Christina, Nick and their little sister, Kelly, had been loved and well taken care of, but their parents were often gone, leaving them in the care of the housekeeper, Franny Fitzgerald. She and her husband, Henry, took care of the estate. Christina loved Franny, but Christina longed for a different life. One where she felt like she had a family.

Not just another obligation. And her parents already had a lot of obligations.

Yet here she was at age thirty, alone. Still. But she loved her cozy house with its brick fireplace that she never used. Why didn't she ever use the fireplace? Curl up with a good book?

A more rational thought came to mind.

Because she was never home.

She probably wouldn't be home now, but Nick had convinced her the paperwork at the clinic could wait for another day. Besides, she hated to impose on him. If she had gone back to work, she would have had to ask for a ride home again later. She really should follow up on her car. See if the sheriff's office had uncovered anything that would determine who had vandalized it. If they weren't going to release it to her, she should consider replacing it. The car was old, it didn't owe her anything. But all the events of late had taken precedence. And if she were being honest, she enjoyed Dylan's company. If she had a car, she wouldn't be able to see his handsome face each morning and evening.

She realized how selfish that sounded.

Rolling her shoulders to ease the knot between her shoulder blades, Christina strolled to the kitchen and flipped on the light. The pretty drop lighting she had installed illuminated the updated kitchen with its oversized gas stove. She put on the teakettle, more out of habit than anything else.

As much as Christina wanted the vandalism of her car to fall into the neat little box labeled, "Roger Everett is a bad man," it didn't make a lot of sense. If Roger was truly worried about her causing him trouble, why would he cause her trouble? Unless he was such a bully that he believed fear controlled everyone.

Hadn't fear controlled her? Wasn't it fear that had kept her from admitting to those closest to her that Roger had attacked her on the beach?

Christina shuddered at the memory of Roger's smug face. How had none of them seen through him from the beginning?

Christina braced her hands on the edge of the counter as she waited for the kettle to whistle. Her mind wandered.

Roger wasn't seen at the barn party, and an adult male in his thirties wouldn't exactly blend in. But did he sneak in and spike a few drinks?

But why Naomi's?

Chance? Or did Naomi's condition have anything to do with this Aaron Webb kid? The boy who may have gotten her pregnant. Was he feeling trapped by a naive Amish girl and wanted to seek retribution? Put doubt in people's minds that he was the father? But DNA tests would quickly resolve paternity if there were doubts. Or was Aaron counting on the Amish not to pursue such medical procedures?

She pressed her fingers to her temple to stem the growing thump, thump, thump.

Was she stretching here? It was a web of tangentially related events. Or maybe they weren't related at all.

Christina's head throbbed as she puzzled at each piece of this strange situation. She yanked the rubber band out of her hair and ran her fingers through it. Normally, she liked working through a problem—mostly a medical concern— but with this, she was coming up blank.

Dylan had offered to sleep outside, in his truck, to protect her, but Christina surprisingly wasn't feeling particularly vulnerable. Not at home. This was her safe haven. It always had been. As a single woman, she'd had an alarm system installed. That in itself had convinced Dylan that she'd be okay. She activated the system at night. She wasn't so much worried about someone breaking in when the house was empty, but she didn't want anyone entering while she was sleeping. The fear of waking up with someone standing over her had been with her since her teenage years, when watching slasher films had seemed like a good idea.

And why come after her here? Dylan knew as much as she did and if something happened to her, Dylan would go right to Roger.

The teakettle emitted a high-pitched whistle and Christina jumped. Maybe she *should* have allowed Dylan to play bodyguard.

She lifted the kettle from the burner, then decided maybe she'd skip her evening tea and instead crawl into bed with a good book. That would help get her mind off her troubles.

Christina secured the house, set the alarm and flipped all the lights off as she made her way down a long hallway to her first-floor bedroom. She pushed open the door, flipped on the light and stopped short. Her brain screamed, "Run! Run! Run!" But a warped sense of bravery, or maybe it was plain old curiosity, had her moving toward the shreds of paper on her bed.

With a shaky hand, she picked up one of the pieces and then another. Matching them up, she recognized her old prescription pad, something she seldom used now since scripts were sent in electronically.

The room went black and a sound exploded behind

her in the dark. Instinctively Christina jumped back and flattened herself against the wall. A dark shadow ran from the bathroom, right toward her. She ducked and scrambled to the alarm panel on the wall. She slammed her hand against it and the strident sounds of the alarm filled the quiet air.

The intruder dove toward the door. Footsteps pounded down the hall. He was fumbling with the locks on the front door now. Christina took that as her cue to slam the bedroom door shut, turning the feeble lock on the handle. Knowing full well the flimsy door wouldn't hold a determined intruder, she slid her cell phone out of her pocket and despite the alarm company's automated response, she called 9-1-1 and waited.

Christina had been a fool to think she was safe.

Dylan made a U-turn as soon as he got the call from Christina's brother. Nick was on his way to Christina's house, but he took a chance that Dylan might be closer, since when he last spoke to Christina she'd told him Dylan was taking her home.

As it turned out, Dylan reached the small cottage first. He grabbed his weapon from the glove box and jumped out of his truck, not bothering to shut the door. His stomach dropped when he heard the strident alarm and noticed Christina's front door ajar, but there was no sign of Christina.

Dylan blinked back the memory of Nora's vacant eyes staring up at him, a pool of blood gathering under her head. He winced and fought to ignore the cord of dread squeezing his throat.

Nora had been as stubborn as Christina, insisting she

was ready for a bigger assignment. He had agreed. A decision he'd forever regret.

Dylan shook off the nightmare that haunted him. Swallowing hard, he lifted his gun and shouldered his way into Christina's dark house, straining to detect any sudden movements in the shadows. The alarm set his nerves further on edge.

He half expected to turn a corner and find Christina in the grip of some crazed lunatic.

What if he was too late? *Again?*

Nick had said Christina reported an intruder to dispatch, but thought the intruder had vacated the property. Nick advised Dylan to proceed with caution if he arrived on the scene first.

Why hadn't she called him directly?

Dylan cleared the family room and kitchen, then stalked down the hallway to where he assumed the bedrooms were located. Only one door was closed. When he reached it, he stood off to the side and turned the handle, in case someone decided to put a few rounds through the doorway. More than one rookie had been caught unaware.

The door was locked.

"Christina?" he called in a harsh whisper. "It's Dylan. Open up."

With a slick palm, he readied the gun in case it wasn't Christina who greeted him at the door.

Through the crack under the door, he noticed the light flick on, then the door slowly opened. Christina fell into his arms in a relieved rush.

Though he was eager to hold her tight, Dylan's training had him setting her aside. "Hold up. Hold up." His arm out in a protective gesture, he did a quick canvass of her room and adjoining bathroom.

When he returned, Christina pressed a few keys on a keypad and the alarm went silent. His ears still rang.

She lowered herself into a white chair in the corner of her bedroom. She held up her hand in a what-do-you-make-of-this? gesture.

Shreds of paper covered her bed.

"My old prescription pad." She answered the question on the tip of his tongue.

Before Dylan had a chance to respond, he heard a commotion at the front door. "Christina's safe. Back bedroom," Dylan called. No sense surprising another law enforcement agency.

Deputy Jennings appeared in the doorway. The tense lines around his eyes eased when he saw his sister was safe, albeit shaken up.

Dylan knew the feeling.

"What happened?" Nick asked.

Another deputy entered the room.

"Whoever decided to make confetti out of my prescription pad was still here when I got home. Made a run for it when I entered the room. I didn't see his face." She angled her head toward the bathroom. "Must have been in there, then flipped the lights off and bolted. All I saw was a shadow."

"You're okay, though?" Nick asked all the questions Dylan wanted to ask.

"Yeah." She turned to Dylan. "How did you know to come?"

"Your brother called me."

Christina turned to Nick, a question in her eyes.

"I thought he might be nearby."

Christina leaned forward and rested her elbows on her

knees, her shoulders sagging. The incident had obviously flustered her. "Thanks for coming. Really."

As if sensing he was intruding on something personal, Nick said, "We'll collect this and see if we can get some prints. Maybe on the door handles. The paper. Whatever. Don't touch anything in the meantime. Grab a few things and you can come home with me."

"Wait!" Christina bristled at being told what to do. "Did you tell Roger about our conversation?" She lowered her voice at the mention of Roger. "Did you confront him? Tell him you knew he had attacked me?"

Nick's face grew red as he rubbed his neck. "I didn't go against your wishes. I know how much you don't want to stir things up with Linda being sick." He gave his little sister a stern look. "Which I don't agree with. I think if Roger attacked you, he needs to be held accountable."

"I agree, but you and I both know you won't be able to hold him for something he's going to deny doing and I have no proof of. Our best hope is to catch him committing another crime." She jabbed a finger at her bed. "If he did this, maybe he was sloppy. Maybe he did leave evidence."

"I haven't spoken to Roger about this." The tight set of his mouth indicated Nick's strain.

Christina sat up ramrod straight and pressed her palm to her forehead. "I'm so stupid."

"What?" Dylan took a step forward. "What is it?"

"Roger's wife Linda was in my office. I asked her if Roger abused her."

"That's not unusual. Physicians ask those kinds of questions." Dylan shifted his stance. "It's part of the reporting system."

"But she got angry." Christina flattened her lips into

a thin line. "Really angry. I don't think she's in Roger's corner as much as she's worried about her son hating his father." She looked out into the middle distance as if she were trying to remember what she had actually said to Linda. "Considering her frail health, I don't think she'd ever tell the truth about Roger. Her son needs a father." Her lower lip quivered. "As much as I can't stand Roger, my heart goes out to Linda." She discreetly wiped at a tear.

She looked up at her brother, then Dylan. "What if Linda told Roger that I asked her if he abused her? Something like that could set him off. He promised he'd make my life miserable if I caused him problems." She held up her palm, indicating the mess.

"You're not safe living alone"

"How did he find the prescription pad?" she asked, as if to herself.

"Where was it?" Nick asked.

"I have a few at home and a few at the office. But I don't use them anymore. We use e-prescriptions."

"You can't stay here," Dylan said.

She shot him a wary gaze. "This is my home."

"I think Dylan's right. You can come and stay with me and Sarah," Nick said.

"I can't impose. You and Sarah have the baby."

Nick smiled. "More like you don't want the baby keeping you up at night."

"Well, there's that, too." A corner of her mouth quirked into a lopsided grin.

Another deputy called for Nick from the other room. Nick held up his finger. "Give me a minute." Then he gave them both a pointed stare. "Don't touch anything."

Dylan studied the determined look on Christina's face

but he could tell it was a brave front. She looked like she was ready to collapse.

"Your brother's right. You really can't stay here."

Christina straightened her spine. "I let Roger silence me with fear. I will not let him run me out of my house. I think it's time we confronted Roger. See what the big bully has to say."

SEVEN

The night of the break-in, Christina's big brother convinced her to hold off on confronting Roger. And he had been right. Nothing productive would have come from pointing her finger at him.

Again, they had no proof.

Or maybe that was her brother's way of keeping her out of harm's way. In any event, a few days had passed and she was working at the clinic, a little tired from sleeping at her brother's house. Who knew babies cried so much? Especially at midnight, two in the morning, four in the morning...

She stifled a yawn. She was grateful for her job. It kept her mind focused on something other than her own concerns.

Right now she was escorting an elderly lady who had come in for a simple blood pressure check to her waiting husband's vehicle. Christina watched as the car pulled away.

She paused and filled her lungs with the sweet air of the beautiful spring day. The sound of the wind rustling the leaves made her want to take a walk. What she wouldn't give to play hooky. It was a strange thought, considering never in her life had she played hooky.

But spending a lot of time with Dylan had created a subtle shift. There were other things to life.

And now she had Georgia to help run the clinic.

She smiled at the notion.

Another yawn snuck up on her and she knew she'd have to find other living arrangements if she hoped to get a good night's sleep. Maybe she should go to her parents' home, but she hated to put out Franny and Henry who took care of the estate. They would surely make a lot of fuss over her.

Or maybe it was the past she didn't want to face.

Christina was opening the door of the clinic when the sound of gravel under tires caught her attention. She spun around to see Georgia in her zippy new red car. Maybe Christina'd get one like that.

Nah, she liked the anonymity of a nondescript car. Function over form.

Christina paused in the doorway and held the door open for Georgia. "Good lunch?"

"Yeah, it was. It was nice to get out for a little bit." She held out her hand, indicating the gorgeous day. "Why don't you go for lunch?" Georgia glanced around Christina into the empty waiting room. "I think I can handle things around here. Go, it's a beautiful day."

"I don't know…" Christina was lost in thought.

"You know I can handle this," Georgia assured her. "And I know how to reach you if something comes up." The competent young woman held up her cell phone. "It's all good." She flicked her hand at her boss in a shoo-shoo gesture, the bangle bracelets on her wrist jangling.

Christina was about to protest when her stomach

grumbled. She could go for a sandwich and the exercise that came with walking the short distance to the diner. Christina peeled off her white coat and walked in to hang it on a hook. "I'll be back in an hour and—"

"If anything comes up, I'll call you." Georgia laughed. "I've got this."

Christina pushed through the front door and smiled as the sun warmed her face. Her feet crunched on the gravel as she crossed the parking lot. This was the first time she'd walked to the diner since the night Ben Reist had almost run her over.

She took a deep breath. That had been an accident. A panicky kid trying to do the right thing by bringing a sick young lady to the clinic. A kid who didn't want to risk his college scholarship by being associated with a young woman who had been drugged.

Christina quickened her pace. Ben nearly running her over. Running into Roger after all these years. Her car being vandalized. Her prescription pad getting shredded and left on her bed…

How were these events connected? How…?

She quickened her pace, hoping the pieces would magically click into place.

The sound of cheers floating from the nearby park pulled her out of her racing mind. Christina glanced over, comforted that she wasn't alone on the country road. A bunch of teenage girls were playing softball. The local schools must have had a half day, today. Christina continued walking when her eye was drawn to a man yelling instructions to the girls.

Roger Everett.

The birds suddenly stopped chirping and a cloud swept across the sun, casting a pall over the otherwise beautiful spring day. Christina shuddered, feeling as if the temperature had dropped considerably.

What was Roger Everett doing? Coaching the girls' softball team? It wouldn't be a stretch. He had been a star baseball player in high school.

She paused and tented her hand over her eyes to double-check what she was seeing. It *was* Roger. And it looked like his son, Matt, was assisting. In good conscience, Christina couldn't stay quiet. But what was she supposed to do?

Then a crazy idea floated to mind. She'd call Dylan to bring her a sandwich. They could sit at the picnic table and watch practice. But she wouldn't be able to stand watch over the girls forever. She'd have to contact the school.

Do something.

It would be just like a predator to put himself in a position to gain access to young women.

Christina fumbled for her phone and called Dylan, grateful he was already on his way to the diner for lunch. She told him to pick her up a sandwich and meet her at the ball diamonds. She'd explain later, but he needed to hurry.

Squaring her shoulders, Christina crossed the street and purposely walked behind the dugout. Her stomach sloshed with unspent adrenaline. What was she doing?

Roger did a double take when he saw her, then a slow smile curved the corners of his thin lips. "You want to take first?"

Christina hadn't planned to say anything to Roger. She wanted to make it abundantly clear that she was watching him. Instead, the heat of anger flushed her face and got the best of her emotions. She turned and hooked her fingers on the chain-link fence separating them. Maybe it gave her a false sense of protection.

"Why is a busy guy like you coaching the girls' softball team?"

He turned around to face her squarely. His lips moved as if to form a word, but then he seemed to back up and change direction. "I hear you treated my wife."

Christina angled her head, slightly taken aback. She neither confirmed nor denied his statement.

"Linda has capable doctors in Buffalo. She doesn't need a small-town doctor who treats cuts and scrapes for a living." His smug expression was infuriating.

Christina swallowed hard and kept her emotions in check. "Your wife needs you. I hope you realize that." Her words held far more meaning than he could possible comprehend.

"What is it you have against me?" He rolled his eyes in a mocking gesture. "Besides that silly misunderstanding we had years ago?" He lowered his voice, checking over his shoulder to find Matt standing across the field close to third base, holding a clipboard and talking to one of the players.

Her anger burned hot and she couldn't think clearly.

"You better not hurt any of these girls." The words flew out of her mouth before she had a chance to think about the ramifications. Then she unhooked her fingers from the chain link and pointed toward the field. The girls were focused on the next batter.

Roger's hands flew up in a surrender gesture. "Now wait a minute. I'm a respected member of this community. How could you…?" He sputtered with rage. Then he took a step closer. Christina stepped back despite the fence separating them.

Roger took off his baseball cap, one whose bill was well worn. "The girls need me. I went to college on a baseball scholarship. I was a big deal."

"So you thought."

Roger gave her a half smile. "A lot of people in Apple Creek thought I was a big deal."

Christina clamped her mouth shut.

"Do me a favor, Dr. Christina. You stay out of my life and I'll stay out of yours. Deal? Because I have the power to cause a lot of problems if you don't."

Christina resisted the urge to shout, "Like what?" But she knew better than to underestimate a bully. Her pulse whooshed slowly through her veins, a steady *no-no-no* in her ears. Roger twisted his lips and glee glinted in his eyes. "What would little old Apple Creek do without their free healthcare clinic?"

It felt like someone had pulled the steel pole out of her spine, but she refused to back down. "You don't have any power over me. Not anymore."

"Hey, Dad." Matt approached from behind, his gaze landing on Christina. "Can I hit a few? Maybe get the team focused on fielding practice?"

The harsh, angry lines immediately smoothed on Roger's face as he turned to his son. "Sure, kiddo. Let's do it." He walked away from Christina and continued the practice as if nothing had transpired between them.

Christina scanned the small parking lot and prayed Dylan would hurry up and get here.

Dear Lord, please help me figure out how to handle this situation. I can't risk Roger hurting one of these young women.

The intensity in Christina's voice had Dylan racing over to the park. He barely had the patience to wait for her order of a turkey club sandwich, but he didn't want her to go hungry. But he had lost his appetite. When he found Christina leaning against the picnic table with her arms tightly crossed, he didn't need to ask her what was wrong. He saw firsthand that Roger Everett was at the park coaching the girls' softball team.

"You're doing surveillance on Roger?" Dylan asked, squinting toward where Roger stood on the sidelines.

"Apparently, Roger got himself a job coaching the girls' softball team."

"How is that possible?"

"Back in his high school days, Roger was a big-deal baseball player. Big deal for a small town. I guess since he's back in town the school hired him to coach the girls' team." Christina pushed away from the picnic table and kicked at the dirt with pent-up frustration. "I can't believe this. He's put himself exactly in a position to harm young girls."

"And your idea was to eat lunch and watch him?" Dylan tried to defuse the heavy situation with a hint of humor.

"It seemed like a good idea until I actually talked to Roger." She shook her head, her jaw clenched as if she were grinding her teeth. "He's the most arrogant person I've ever met. I think he thinks that because he was hot stuff in high school, he can come back here and is untouchable."

"Usually, it's the arrogant criminals who get caught."

Christina reached into the white bag and pulled out a foam container. She looked up, a question in her eyes. "Didn't you get yourself something to eat?"

"No, I'm fine." He was too anxious to think about eating after Christina had called him.

She seemed to consider that a moment, then popped open the lid. He almost wished he'd grabbed something when the smell of bacon wafted in his direction. She picked at a piece of bacon poking out of the edge of her sandwich. "My brother's quietly investigating Roger. It's a weak case, but I know what he did to me and I can't risk him doing it to one of these girls. Doing worse."

Dylan sat on the picnic bench next to her, facing away from the table. He leaned his elbows on the rugged surface, forcing her to look at him. "What do you want to do?"

She chewed on a bite of her sandwich thoughtfully. "What are our options?"

"Sometimes past experience colors our outlook." Dylan ran his hand across his chin. He had been blinded when it came to nailing the guys who killed his partner. He had almost killed an innocent when he set out for revenge for his partner's death. Not justice. He didn't want Christina to go down the same path.

"You sound like you're talking from experience." Christina's words snapped him out of his reverie.

Dylan shrugged. "I might have heard it on Dr. Phil once." He wasn't ready to open up to Christina about the nightmare that had led him away from the FBI. He didn't want anger to cloud her judgment as it had his.

They needed to proceed objectively.

Dylan closed his eyes briefly, assessing the situation. "If you want Roger put away, law enforcement needs to build a case. You can't let your emotions get the best of you."

Christina roughly flipped the foam lid down on her takeout container. "I agree." She held out her open palm toward the girls playing softball. "But what do I do in the meantime? Wait to treat his next victim?"

"That doesn't seem like an appealing option."

"No, it doesn't."

Dylan shifted to see whatever had caught Christina's attention. The softball team cleared the field and headed toward the gray van with the words *Apple Creek Central School District* painted on the side. This was worse than a cliché. A bunch of young ladies getting into a van with a creep.

Roger continued to talk with one of the girls as they passed. Only Matthew, Roger's son, slowed down. "What do you have against my dad?"

"We're having a little lunch here," Dylan lied, feeling it was justified.

Matt crossed his arms and glared at Christina. "You were arguing with my dad. Not just today, but at my house."

Christina held on to the edge of the picnic table, stood, pulling one leg, then the other over the bench. A war of indecision played across Christina's face. "This is an adult matter."

Roger's son seemed to flinch.

Christina ran a hand over her mouth. "How's your mom?"

Matt's entire body language shifted from being a confident young man to a worried little boy. "She didn't get out of bed this morning. My dad offered to take her to the hospital, but she said she didn't want to go. She gets car sick."

"Do you know where the Apple Creek clinic is? You can bring your mom to the clinic if she wants to come, right? She told me you have a license. That's not too far to drive."

Dylan wasn't surprised by Christina's compassion, even when it came to the wife of a man she apparently hated.

"Come on, son," Roger called. "You're making everyone wait."

Matt tipped his head toward the van, as if to say, "I gotta go." The teenager jogged away without a word or a backward glance.

Christina plopped back down on the bench next to Dylan, both of their backs propped up against the thin edge of the picnic table.

"What do you make of that? Do you think Matt knows what's going on?" Christina got a faraway look as she watched the van pull away. "Do you think he knows his father's a creep?"

"Sons want to look up to their fathers." Dylan left it at that. He'd wanted more than anything to respect his own father, but the man had proven that not every father deserved a son's admiration.

EIGHT

Georgia was proving to be invaluable at the clinic, which allowed Christina to go with Dylan to the high school the next afternoon.

Christina had a fine line on which to balance. She wanted to warn the school about Roger, yet she had no proof. Would Roger sue her for slander? She understood the seriousness of making accusations, something she as a physician had to worry about herself. Angry people said angry things.

But the well-being of the young girls won out over what might have been prudent. She thought about calling her brother, but decided taking the unofficial approach was better than getting the sheriff's office involved because, again, she had no solid evidence against Roger, other than her own experience. And that incident was ripe for he said, she said.

Christina's stomach knotted as they sat in the small waiting room outside Mrs. Acer's office. Principal Acer had been the principal when Christina was a student at Apple Creek High School.

Christina felt like she was a student again, caught in indecision. She stared out the tall windows, watching black clouds gathering in the distance. There was something very apropos about that.

Christina wrapped her hand around her umbrella and lifted it slightly. "Good thing I grabbed my umbrella before I left home. Looks like, for once, the weather forecasters might be right."

"Yeah," Dylan said, his mood somber.

Christina leaned closer as they sat on the bench and bumped his shoulder. "This has to be done." Roger coaching young women—little older than girls—was *not* a good idea.

He gave her a reassuring nod.

"Why, hello, Dr. Christina Jennings." The distinguished fiftysomething principal appeared in the doorway with a surprised expression on her face.

"Principal Acer." Christina stood. A strong sense of nostalgia washed over her and she had to resist the urge to pull this woman into a fierce hug. She had done much to shape Christina's future. Principal Acer had been the one Christina bounced ideas off, since her own parents had spent her senior year expanding one of their business ventures into France. Or maybe Germany. Portugal? Inwardly she shook her head. Either way, Christina had learned to rely on other adults in her life.

Principal Acer held out her arms, warmth and welcome rolling off her in waves. "To what do I owe the pleasure, Dr. Jennings?" The woman always called her Dr. Jennings whenever they ran into each other at the diner or elsewhere in town. It was as if she had raised hundreds of young men and woman and cherished each of their successes, and tried hard not to harp on their failures.

"I hate to bother you. I know you're gearing up for final exams and everything."

Principal Acer glanced at the wall clock, the ubiquitous round white clock with black numbers. Christina wondered if there was a store that supplied these clocks to schools across the country. Yet she found many of her youngest patients couldn't tell time when looking at a traditional clock.

"Come in." Principal Acer paused and held her hand out to Dylan.

"Oh, how rude of me." Christina stopped. "This is my friend, Dylan Hunter. He's a professor at the university and on sabbatical from the FBI."

The principal took his hand, a worried look crossing her features. "FBI? I hope you don't have bad news for me."

"Can we go into your office?" Christina asked, noticing the young secretary glanced at them with a look of curiosity. She didn't know the woman, but feared the gossip that might spread like fire across dry wood if dropped in the wrong spot.

"Sure, sure." The principal turned to the secretary. "Hold my calls."

"Sure thing."

The three of them went into the office. A large window overlooked the huge playground of the elementary school on the adjacent property. Christina vaguely remembered buying candy bars or something to support the PTA's fundraising efforts for a new playground, pushing the whole kids-need-to-be-more-active-and-have-less-screen-time mantra that was generally a good idea. However, Christina wondered if anyone else saw the irony in selling candy bars. No matter, she enjoyed milk chocolate as much as the next person.

"Playground turned out nice," Christina said, sitting in one of the two chairs facing the principal's desk.

The older woman glanced out the window over her shoulder. "We're grateful." She smiled. "Maybe now the PTA parents can fundraise for a soundproof office. Have you ever heard fifty little children letting off steam at recess? It's as if screaming is a release valve." She shuddered at the memory of it. "There was a reason I chose to work in a high school. Can't help that the elementary building is next door."

"It's wonderful they're able to have recess," Christina said, feeling like the polite conversation had dragged on perhaps a moment too long.

Principal Acer sat down and rested her elbows on her desk, obviously feeling the same way. "What brings you to Apple Creek High School?"

Christina glanced over at Dylan, grateful for his support.

"I understand you hired Roger Everett to coach the girls' softball team."

"Yes…" The simply word hung out there like a question she feared the answer to.

"Do you do background checks on all your employees?" Dylan asked before the principal had a chance to say more. But even Christina understood a background check wouldn't detect a crime if someone had gotten away with it.

Principal Acer squared her shoulders. "We fingerprint our employees. Require them to take Child Abuse and Violence Abuse workshops. It's New York State policy. Anyone who works with the children in our schools has this required training." She shuffled around a few papers. "The opening for the coaching position came up rather suddenly." Her voice grew hesitant. "Coach Gaulbert had a family emergency. We were lucky Coach Everett happened to move back to town. His family is well respected in the community. The school board appointed him to the interim position unanimously."

"Does this mean you didn't run the required background checks?" Dylan asked, pointedly.

Goose bumps blanketed Christina's arms as she waited for the principal to answer Dylan's question. A small part of her felt like she was being disrespectful to her former principal. Sometimes it took time to shift from the teacher–student relationship to that of peers. Sitting on this side of the principal's desk definitely put Christina at a disadvantage. Funny how a place—her eyes drifted to Dylan, who was focused on Principal Acer—or a person could immediately take you back to another time. Another place.

The deep lines around the principal's mouth spoke more than her calm words. "I'd have to look in our files, but I'm sure everything's in place. It's merely a formality."

Roger's smug expression floated to mind. Christina couldn't back down now. She scooted forward onto the edge of her chair. "Roger Everett is not a good fit to coach the girls' softball team." A hot wave of unease washed over her.

"What?" Principal Acer leaned back in the leather chair, which gave off a high-pitched screech.

"When I was in college, Roger attacked me."

"Roger attacked you?" The principal repeated in an uncertain tone. "He's such a nice young man. Respected in our community. His father is the former mayor."

Out of the corner of her eye, she noticed Dylan leaning toward her as if he wanted to say something to her, but she kept her focus on the principal. Christina couldn't lose her nerve now.

"He's a real peach," Christina said with an edge to her tone.

"Do you have proof? I mean, I can't fire him on your say-so."

Christina dragged her hand through her hair. "I'm afraid it would be my word against his. But I wouldn't come here with the accusation unless my concerns were real." She tapped her fingers on the edge of the desk, trying to think of a more direct solution. "Perhaps all his paperwork is not complete according to NYS. Maybe you could postpone his appointment. Tell him his paperwork's not in order. It could buy us—well, the sheriff's department—time to look into his background."

Principal Acer pivoted in her chair. Her porcelain skin had gone even whiter. She stared out the window as if deep in thought. When the principal didn't say anything, Christina added, "I'm worried about the girls…" Niggling doubt immediately wormed its way into her brain. He had undoubtedly attacked her, but what else was he guilty of?

Christina sat back in her chair and crossed her arms tightly around her. "Roger Everett attacked me. *That* I know for sure." Christina's voice got very low and the walls in the room swayed. She suddenly got very hot.

"Christina felt she needed to tell you about her past with Roger Everett to protect the young women on the softball team," Dylan spoke up. "In good conscience, she couldn't keep her mouth closed."

Not anymore.

Principal Acer turned her attention to him. "Has this

become an FBI matter?" A deep line marred her forehead. "Is there an official investigation?"

"I'm on leave from the FBI. I'm here as a personal friend of Christina's."

Christina turned to look at him. The regret in his tone was unmistakable. "Dylan is an old friend." She gave him a half smile. "My brother, Nick, is aware of my concerns. The sheriff's department is watching Roger closely. But, please, keep that to yourself."

Principal Acer shifted in her seat to face them squarely. "If I remember correctly, your brother and Roger were good friends."

"Yes, yes they are."

Principal Acer twisted her lips. "That must be hard."

"Yes, and I fear my brother's friendship with Roger made me keep my mouth shut for far too many years. Who knows how many other women he attacked?"

Principal Acer wrapped her hands around the arms of her oversized black chair. "Tell you what. I'll contact Coach Everett and tell him he needs to have an assistant coach with him at all times until he's completed all his workshops and has been fingerprinted. I'll word it such that it's all bureaucratic stuff." The corners of her mouth turned down. "The school board will also have to be notified that he can't coach alone. Not until his paperwork is done."

"The school board won't like it," Christina warned.

Principal Acer folded her hands and looked at Christina pointedly. "I imagine they won't. Coach Everett might not like having someone looking over his shoulder, either. The man is a great athlete, but he can be a hothead."

Fingers of unease squeezed at her throat. "Once Roger knows I reported him, he's not going to be happy."

"Our students' safety is more important than a man's pride. If Coach Everett has nothing to hide, he'll understand we have to follow protocol." Principal Acer shook the mouse and her computer screen came to life. She clicked a few buttons. "I'll assign someone to work with him today."

Principal Acer squinted at the computer screen for a moment before turning to glance out the window. The first wet drops of rain hit the window panes. "Well, looks like we might have dodged a bullet today. Practice will be cancelled on account of the rain. It will give me time to make a few phone calls, find a temporary volunteer to help coach the team, preferably a member of our staff who already has their information on file."

"Thank you," Christina said, feeling a sense of relief.

"Thank you for coming forward. I can see that it wasn't easy." Principal Acer smiled, but sadness lit her eyes.

Lately, nothing had been easy.

Christina had to take large steps to keep up with Dylan as they strode down the long, mostly empty corridors of the very school she attended. The authoritative voices of teachers finishing up their lessons for the day floated out of various classroom doors as they passed. The high school year ran a good month longer than the university's calendar year.

The more she thought of the principal's temporary fix, the more she didn't like it. Roger was sneaky. He could find a way to be alone with one of the girls.

"How can we leave it like that?" Christina asked, her

voice hushed. "Roger's going to hurt one of those girls. I can feel it in my bones."

Dylan took her hand and pulled her toward the main doors. Through the windows she could see that a line of yellow buses had formed, their black numbers hard to read in the driving rain. Dylan turned to face her, placing both his hands on her shoulders. "I understand how important this is to you. But the principal is in a difficult situation. She can't fire Roger on our say-so. There needs to be due process. I think we accomplished our goal of warning her. She'll be watching him. An assistant coach will be watching him. Usually that's enough to give a guy like Roger pause. He's not dumb."

"Some comfort to the girl he hurts." Christina shifted her stance and glanced behind Dylan through the window to the gloomy weather. Good, she thought, it suited her mood.

"The school board didn't even wait for Roger to complete all the requirements. They could probably get in trouble for that," Christina whispered. "Can't we use that?" Her mind was swirling. They had to do *something.* Especially after having not done anything for far too long. A familiar niggling of guilt pinged her insides. She forced it aside, knowing in her heart—even if not always in her head—that she had kept quiet for reasons that had made sense at the time.

She had been the victim.

Dylan angled his head. "Do you really think that's the best way to proceed? To put the principal on the defensive? Perhaps put her job in jeopardy?"

Christina bowed her head and sighed heavily. "I feel helpless." Much like she had felt after Roger had viciously attacked her and she didn't know where to turn.

An unintended consequence of Roger's actions had been that Christina focused with laser-like intensity on school and now her career. After getting her heart broken by Dylan and her spirit crushed by Roger, she didn't trust herself beyond the realm in which she excelled, one she could control.

"Maybe I should have Nick approach Roger. If he realizes the number of people watching him, maybe he'll stay honest. Maybe." She let out a long breath.

"I'll help you. I promise." Dylan offered her a comforting smile. His smooth voice warmed her soul. How could this be the same man who so callously dumped her?

A lifetime ago. Wasn't it long past time that she forgave him?

A crash of thunder made her jump. Dylan laughed and dropped his hands from her shoulders.

Christina shook her head. "Man, I'm jumpy."

Dylan glanced behind him. "That lightning strike was close." The wind whipped sideways and raindrops whooshed against the window. "Looks like we're going to get wet."

"Remember, I have my umbrella."

He laughed. Her umbrella was unlikely to keep anyone totally dry in this monsoon.

The sound of her phone ringing in her purse caught her attention over the raging storm outside. Her mind immediately went to the clinic. "I better take this call."

Dylan nodded as he pushed open the door and held his hand to the storm. "We're not going anywhere, anyway."

Christina smiled and swiped across the face of the phone, accepting the call. She didn't recognize the number. "Hello?"

Sobbing sounded over the line.

"Hello?" Christina repeated.

"It's me, Naomi."

Christina's heart sank. "What's wrong?"

"I can't take it anymore. I need to know."

The ticking of the clock slowed as she waited for her Amish friend to continue.

"I need to figure out my future." Naomi's voice grew very soft. "Can I come into the clinic for one of those tests?" A pregnancy test.

"Of course. Of course." Christina turned her back to Dylan who didn't seem to be listening anyway. "When do you want to come in?"

"As soon as possible. Are you at the clinic now? Cheryl can drive me over."

"No, I'm at the school."

If Naomi was surprised Christina was at the school, she didn't let on.

"My friend Cheryl told me we can get a test at the store, but I'd feel better..."

"Of course." The home pregnancy tests were highly accurate. However, if Naomi was pregnant, she'd need prenatal care. Christina didn't want to dismiss her in exchange for a test she could buy at the local pharmacy for under ten dollars.

Christina said a silent prayer that the young Amish woman would trust Christina even as the potential for Naomi's world imploding loomed heavy, like the ominous dark clouds.

Christina glanced over at Dylan. "I can be at the clinic in ten minutes. Does that work?"

Dylan silently gestured his understanding. He leaned toward the umbrella in Christina's hand. "I'll pull up the car on the other side of the buses," he mouthed. "Wait here."

Just as he said that, the school bell rang its shrill *bring*, a sound that had probably remained constant since the founders laid the school cornerstone.

"Hold on." Christina spoke into the phone and pressed against the wall as the students filled the halls, like popped popcorn escaping a hot kettle.

"I'm going," Dylan hollered over the cacophony of students chattering, locker doors slamming and sneakers skidding across the marble floor.

Christina covered one ear so she could hear Naomi and was only peripherally aware of Dylan pushing on the solid school doors and opening her colorful floral umbrella. It had been a gift from her mother and Christina was relieved it hadn't been destroyed when Ben Reist nearly flattened her during the near miss in the clinic parking lot.

"Naomi," Christina said into the phone, "I'll be at the clinic in ten minutes. I'll help you however I can."

Naomi hiccupped over the line. "Okay. *Denki.*"

Christina paused long enough to be sure her friend had hung up. The bus loop in front of the school was crowded with vehicles. From her vantage point inside the doors at the top of a long flight of stairs, she saw her floral umbrella dodging between the students, some with umbrellas, others with their hoods pulled up and even more ignoring the rain as they got soaked.

Feeling a little silly for making Dylan run out to the car—the rain had let up a bit—Christina hustled down the stairs, stepping carefully so as not to tumble down the slick pavement, weaving between the students eager to get to the bus or their cars and get home. She missed that feeling of excitement, knowing a weekend was coming up. How long had it been since she relaxed?

A bolt of lightning split the black clouds and Christina flinched. The darkness made it seem much later than three o'clock in the afternoon. She glanced toward the crowded bus loop now teeming with students and a half dozen buses. She had lost sight of the umbrella.

Suddenly a loud scream rose above the chatter of high school students. Her heart thundered in her chest and panic made her blood run cold. Her eyes darted around. The crowd was filled with young men in baseball caps and hoodies and young women in boots and leggings. A smattering of umbrellas dotted the scene.

Where was Dylan?

Urgency had her barreling down the stairs. She had to grab the railing when she lost her footing on the slick stairs, just as she feared. She nearly yanked her arm out of its socket. She groaned and righted herself.

A crowd of students pushed and shoved between two buses. Instinctively, Christina followed the commotion. She finally broke through the crowd and found Dylan lying on the pavement, eyes closed, her floral umbrella tumbling across the parking lot on a gust of wind.

Feeling nauseous, she dropped to her knees at his side. "Dylan…what happened?" She glanced around but didn't see anything out of the ordinary. She touched his neck and relief thrummed through her in time with his steady pulse. She turned around and stared at the students. A few had the nerve to take photos with their smartphones.

"Call the police. We need an ambulance." Her voice was laced with anger and fear.

Leaning over Dylan, she pulled her arms out of her jacket and placed it over him to keep him warm.

Dear Lord, please let Dylan be okay.

Pointing at the closest student, she said, "Did you dial 9-1-1?"

The girl nodded, her eyes wide with fear.

"Thank you." She checked his pulse again. *Steady.* She swallowed hard and held out her arm. "Move back. Give him some room."

NINE

The last thing Dylan remembered was waving to Christina, then checking around the bus for traffic. Finding the road clear, he'd tilted his umbrella to block the wind and rain and started jogging toward the car parked in the lot beyond the bus loop. Then he'd heard an engine race, tires squeal. He lifted his umbrella and he saw the headlights of a car in the rain gunning for him.

Instinctively Dylan dived and that's all she wrote.

Next thing he knew, he was waking up looking into Christina's warm eyes. "Shhh…" she said when he tried to talk. "The paramedics are here. They'll take you to the hospital. I'll follow behind. My brother's here, too."

"How long was I out?" Dylan groaned.

"Long enough for help to arrive." Christina stepped back and allowed the paramedic to put his kit down and kneel next to Dylan. "His pulse is steady, but he lost consciousness."

"I'm okay." Dylan shook his head. *Big mistake.* Pain ripped through his skull.

Despite Christina's insistence that he stay still, he pushed to a seated position and handed her the jacket she had draped over him. The rain soaked through his jeans. He dragged a hand through his wet hair. "Did you see anything?"

"You need to let this paramedic do his job," Christina said.

"I need to know what's going on."

Christina turned to the paramedic, biting back her frustration. "Give me a minute, okay?"

The young man nodded and took a step back.

Christina crouched down next to Dylan. "What happened?"

"I'm not sure. I heard tires squealing. I saw headlights in the rain." Dylan squinted. "I couldn't tell you the make or model." His voice was gruff.

"I heard the commotion. The buses were in the way." Christina pivoted on the wet pavement, looking around. "Nick's already interviewing the students. The staff."

"Did you tell him why we were here?" Dylan cleared his throat, trying not to sound as disoriented as he felt.

"Yeah, I had to. Otherwise he'd be wondering. I think he's upset we went around him, but I couldn't risk Roger hurting one of the girls on the softball team."

"Of course."

A young girl ran over and handed Christina the umbrella. Christina smiled up at her, grateful for the thoughtful gesture.

Principal Acer moved through the crowd, directing the last few kids to board their respective buses. "Time to get moving," she hollered and gently nudged a young man who appeared to be videotaping the scene. "Your parents will be calling the school wondering why your bus is late." Her monotone voice suggested she had made this plea before, albeit under different circumstances.

Dylan started to get to his feet when Christina held

out her hand. "No, don't get up. You probably have a concussion. The paramedics will take you to the hospital for more tests."

Dylan stumbled to his feet and Christina mumbled something about him not following directions. She draped his arm around her waist to steady him, not a small feat for her tiny frame. But he wasn't about to argue. He liked the way she smelled, of fresh rain and an undercurrent of something...cucumbers. He smiled at that, wondering if he had hit his head harder than he thought.

The bus engines revved and Christina guided Dylan farther away as the buses rumbled out of the parking lot.

"They'll have an earful for their parents tonight." He rubbed his head. "I wonder if any of them saw anything?"

"Let Nick worry about that."

Dylan groaned at the paramedic who took him by the elbow. "I'm not going to the hospital."

"You need to." Christina took his other arm and guided him to the back of the ambulance.

"You're a doctor." Dylan playfully rested his cheek on the top of her head. "You can take care of me."

"They'll need to run tests. See if anything is broken. I don't have those facilities at the clinic."

"Nothing is broken. I've broken bones. I know broken bones. Nothing's broken."

Christina shot him a skeptical look and helped him sit on the edge of the ambulance. She did a few tests on him to see if he was showing signs of a concussion and based on her intense expression he probably did have one. No surprise to him, since his head was killing him.

She frowned. "You need to go to the hospital. A head injury is a big deal."

"You can watch me. Make sure I'm okay."

"How you doing there?" He looked up to see Nick strolling over.

Dylan rubbed his head. "I've been better." He pushed to his feet and immediately regretted it as dizziness swirled around his head. The paramedic put a hand on his shoulder and made him sit back down. He shone a penlight in Dylan's eyes then moved his finger in front of him.

"The doctor's right. Looks like you have a concussion."

Dylan held up his hand. "Hold up." He turned to Nick. "Did any of these kids see anything?"

Nick shook his head. "No one's talking. The principal's giving me a list of names. We can track them down, check their social media sites, see what comes up."

Dylan nodded his agreement and was immediately sorry. *Oh, my aching head.*

Christina disappeared and after a few minutes of the paramedics poking him, he'd had enough. "I'm fine. I'm going home with Dr. Christina Jennings." He pointed at Christina.

Before she had a chance to protest, he gave her a pleading look. "I'm not going to the hospital," he repeated, this time for her benefit.

Christina stepped forward. "I've got this patient. I'm a doctor. I can take you to my parents' home on the escarpment. Keep an eye on you."

The paramedic nodded, not that he agreed, but rather that he'd been there before. "You have to sign an AMA form." Against Medical Advice. He walked over to the ambulance, retrieved a clipboard and shoved it into Dylan's hands.

Dylan signed it. "Here you go."

He started to make his way toward Nick, but Christina grabbed his arm. "Not so fast. If you want me to take responsibility for you, you're going home to take it easy."

"Let me touch base with Nick first."

"You're an awful patient."

He couldn't help but smile. "But you're an amazing doctor."

He gazed into her beautiful brown eyes and once again couldn't remember what he had been thinking when he broke things off with her in college. The only thing he could come up with was that he'd been a fool.

A constant *ding-ding-ding* scraped across her nerves as Christina put Dylan's truck in reverse and maneuvered out of the parking spot. She put the gear in Drive and squinted at the D, wondering why she was having so much trouble.

"Are you sure you can drive this thing?" Dylan asked.

Christina put her foot on the brake and glared at him. "Don't you trust me with your precious baby?" The adrenaline surge from earlier had ebbed and left her feeling grumpy.

"Um…" Dylan pointed at the dash. "You need to release the parking brake."

Christina felt her face flush and she leaned over to try to see where she was supposed to disengage the brake. "Ahhh…" she muttered to herself and pressed the brake pedal to release it. "I see you're feeling better." Her tone was laced with sarcasm.

"I told you I was fine." His voice was strong but she noticed him wince.

"Head hurt?"

"Yeah," he said, finally being honest.

Christina navigated her way out onto the main road. It didn't take her long to get accustomed to driving a vehicle that felt twice the size of hers, the one that was probably sitting in a junkyard right now waiting to be scrapped after it was vandalized. She *really* needed to see about a new car.

Christina tapped her fingers on the steering wheel. "What do you think happened back there?"

"I don't know. I let my guard down."

"We were in the school talking to the principal about Roger Everett. Who knew we were there?"

"I don't know." Dylan tugged on the seat belt.

"Does your arm hurt?"

"I'm fine," he said again, this time with an edge of annoyance in his tone. "Maybe we should go pay Roger a visit."

"No, you need to rest. Nick can follow up. And don't forget I'm the doctor. You won't convince me as easily as you did the paramedics that you're fine."

"They made me sign a release."

"They're smart. I should force you to go to the hospital right now."

"You're a doctor. Why do I need to go to a hospital?"

Christina slowed at the intersection and looked both ways.

"Because I don't like difficult patients." She cut him a sideways glance. She couldn't help but notice the way he held his arm close to his chest.

Christina's phone dinged. "Can you check that?" She never answered her phone when she was driving.

"You don't mind me going into your purse?"

Christina rolled her eyes. "Would you just check my phone, *please*?"

With one hand, Dylan plopped her bag on his lap and unzipped it. He reached in and pulled out her phone. "It's from Cheryl, it says—"

"Ah, man, I forgot about Naomi. I need to get to the clinic. What does the message say?"

"'We're at the clinic. Where are you?'"

"With all the commotion, Cheryl and Naomi beat me to the clinic. Naomi had called just before I left the school building. She wanted to come in." Christina glanced over at Dylan. "Do you mind? It won't take long. Actually, I can pick up some pain meds for you while I'm there."

"Do what you have to do."

A few minutes later they arrived at the clinic. Cheryl's orange sedan sat in the parking lot. Naomi emerged from the passenger side, her bonneted head bowed, and she ran toward the door to meet Christina. The Amish woman's furtive actions reminded Christina of how delicate this matter was.

Christina had already opened a can of worms with one of the town's returning war heroes. She didn't want to do the same for Naomi, who only seemed to want to carve out a peaceful life with the Amish after making a foolish decision.

Naomi opened her mouth to say something when she noticed Dylan sauntering up with Cheryl right behind. Christina held out her hand and opened the door. "Come inside. We'll have privacy there."

Christina turned to Dylan. "Have a seat in my office. It's quiet in there. I won't be long. And Cheryl, if you don't mind you can wait in the waiting room."

"No problem," Cheryl said, casually.

Christina led Naomi to the back of the clinic. "Hello, Georgia, how's everything going here?"

"Good. Had a few patients earlier, but it's been quiet."

"How we like it, right?"

Georgia smiled and nodded her head toward Christina's office. "What's going on?"

"Almost got hit by a car." Dylan's voice was even, steady, not really the tone of a person who had recently been knocked unconscious.

Georgia's eyes flared wide. "What in the world is going on here in Apple Creek? The world's gone crazy."

Worry creased the corners of Naomi's eyes. "Excuse me." Christina held out her hand to guide Naomi into an exam room.

"I'll only be a few minutes."

"Take your time." Dylan went into her office and sat down.

Christina closed the exam door. Naomi was standing in the middle of the room with her hands clasped in front of her. All her innocence and naiveté rolled off of her. Preoccupied, Christina rubbed her arms, wondering how it was possible that sweet Naomi could have been so reckless.

An hour later, a million conflicting emotions washed over Christina when her parents' house—her childhood home—came into view. It was on a beautiful piece of land that overlooked the escarpment in an otherwise flat countryside. It was located ten minutes from the center of Apple Creek and an hour from Buffalo. A perfect getaway. Yet her parents rarely stayed here, instead choosing to travel the world.

It had taken some convincing, but Dylan finally realized she wasn't bluffing when she said he had to stay overnight at her parents' house under her care or she was going to drag him into the ER. So, after a couple quick stops to pick up a change of clothes, they were finally here.

"Wow, *this* is where you grew up?" Dylan leaned forward and stared up at the house through the windshield of his truck.

"Yes." What more could she say? She'd never brought friends here even though she went to the public high school in town. She'd figured it would change the way people thought of her. Of course, there was often speculation, but she preferred that to confirmation.

Christina parked in the circular driveway between the fountain and the impressive double doors. "You want the emergency brake on?" she asked with an edge of humor.

"I think the truck will be okay."

"Come on. You should rest." She pushed open the door and walked around to his side of the truck to help him out.

"I got it." He seemed to be favoring his right arm. "You don't need to help me."

Christina shrugged. "Whatever suits you." She reached around him and slammed the truck door closed all the same. She walked slowly to the front door, waiting for Dylan to catch up.

"I don't need to rest, but it's not a bad idea to hole up here. I'd feel better if I knew you were safe. Someone already had access to your house."

"Ha." Christina entered a code on the front door and it opened. "I brought you here so I could keep an eye on you and your concussion. Don't turn this around as if you're doing me a favor." They'd be more comfortable at her parents' estate, never mind the fact she didn't want to get any tongues wagging. And her brother's place was too small to accommodate them all.

A slow smile curved his mouth, transforming his whole face. He really needed to smile more often. "Okay, we're doing each other a favor."

Christina pushed open the door and noticed the awe that registered on Dylan's face. "Wow. What exactly do your parents do, again?"

Christina lifted a shoulder. "They're entrepreneurs. If you really want to know what they do, you'll have to ask my little sister, Kelly. She's the only one who went into the family business. She could explain it better." She paused a moment, thinking about it. "Or I suppose you could Google them. Jennings Enterprises."

"Interesting. And you became a physician and your brother's in law enforcement." He craned his neck to take in the soaring ceilings in the foyer.

"My parents always encouraged us to follow our dreams. And due to my parents' generosity, the clinic has stayed in the black. I'm very fortunate to be able to practice medicine in Apple Creek and not have to worry about finances." Worry to excess, that is. Christina still pinched pennies, knowing that her parents might not always be an open stream of money.

Dylan nodded and winced as he held his arm close to his body.

"You should have had X-rays done at the hospital."

"I already told you—"

"How wonderful to see you, Dr. Christina."

Christina turned to see Franny Fritzgerald striding across the marble foyer. She held out her hands and cupped Christina's cheeks. Christina had called ahead out of courtesy. She didn't want to presume it was a convenient time to show up. "You don't come around here enough."

"I'm afraid I've been busy at the clinic."

"Always busy." Franny rolled her eyes, but in a playful manner.

Franny and her husband, Henry, had taken care of her parents' house for the past thirty years. Franny was like a second mother to Christina and her siblings.

The older woman turned to Dylan. "And this is your friend, Dylan. *Finally* we get to meet."

The word "finally" held far more weight than it should have carried. Renewed worry wormed its way in and pressed heavily on Christina's heart. "Someone seems to have an issue with me, and maybe Dylan. Can you make sure you keep the doors locked and the alarm set? I'd hate to bring any trouble to your doorstep."

Franny opened her eyes wide, but didn't seem overly concerned. "Your parents always made sure this home was secure. But you're not going to get off that easy. You're going to have to tell me what's going on." Franny pursed her lips and clucked, like the mother hen she was.

"Someone tried to run Dylan over. The driver may have been aiming for me, because Dylan was holding my umbrella at an odd angle to block the blowing rain." She cut a sideways glance at Dylan who had obviously been thinking the same thing.

"Who would do such a thing?" Franny asked, clutching the fabric of her crisp white blouse.

"The sheriff's department is investigating." Christina wanted to blurt out *Roger Everett*, but she decided to keep it to herself. They had no real evidence other than that he was jerk who had gone after her.

And how many others? That familiar haunting voice nagged Christina.

Christina stepped back and let her hand linger near

the doorknob. "Maybe it was a bad idea to come here." She'd never forgive herself if Franny or Henry were hurt because of her.

Would Roger really go that far? What would be the point?

Another dark thought hit her and she gasped. She had heard of guys coming back from the war with anger issues. Was that what had happened to Roger? When he first attacked her, he had already been on one deployment and was ready to go off on a second.

Dylan was still babying his arm, something he'd immediately stop doing if she dared call him on it again.

"No, no...this place is very safe. We always set the alarm. The world is a crazy place and Henry and I are responsible for this home." She held out her palms as if to emphasize *this* home. "You both can stay here as long as you'd like."

"Do you think maybe Henry can park Dylan's truck in the garage? I'd rather not advertise that we're staying here."

"What's going on, dear? This is so unlike you. You've got me worried." Franny's forehead furrowed, much like it had when Christina used to tell her about the mean girls at school or the test she thought she had failed, all made better by homemade cookies and tea.

"We're not quite sure, but there have been a few incidents," Dylan said.

"It's nothing," Christina quickly added. "It'll pass."

"Okay," Franny said, stretching the word out in three syllables. "You're the only one I've never had to worry about. What with your brother putting himself in harm's way in the sheriff's department and your little sister traveling the world… I always took some measure of comfort knowing you're right here in Apple Creek."

Christina stifled a wince, wondering not for the first time if her fear of opening herself up had led to a life that was smaller than it could have been.

Franny held out her hand and Christina frowned. "The keys," Franny said, by way of explanation, "to move the truck."

"Oh…" Christina laughed and handed them over.

"Thanks for your hospitality," Dylan said. He pointed to his head. "The doctor has to keep an eye on me because she doubts how hard my head is."

"Oh, if the doctor thinks you need looking after, you need looking after. She's one smart doctor."

The corners of Dylan's mouth tugged down in mock uncertainty.

"I suppose I need to give you more information because I don't want to put you and Henry in danger." This all still seemed surreal.

"What is it?" Franny studied her, much like she had when Christina came home from college the weekend after Dylan broke up with her claiming that nothing was wrong.

"There's something I never told you."

"Oh," Franny said with a hurt tone.

"I never told anyone." The back of her throat ached. "Remember Roger Everett?"

"Your brother's friend…?"

Christina nodded. "I should have said something a long time ago…" She paused, deciding she was too tired to go into all the details about the attack back when she was in college. Franny might somehow blame herself. Women were good at that. "I can give you more information later, but Dylan and I have had a few near misses and I think Roger is behind them." *Maybe.*

Franny shook her head. "I don't know what this world is coming to." She stepped forward and cupped Christina's cheek with her warm, soft hand. "But one thing I do know. If you say Roger's not welcome around here, he's not."

Franny's quick acceptance of her word as truth filled Christina with an emotion she couldn't quite name. Maybe she hadn't trusted those closest to her to be accepting. Tears filled her eyes and she quickly looked away.

Christina cleared her throat. "Come on, Dylan, I'll show you your room, then we can order a pizza or something." She lowered her voice. "Come up with a plan."

"Sound good," Dylan said.

Franny lifted her hands. "You're not ordering pizza. I'll make you your favorite."

"You don't have to."

"My pleasure. Henry and I rattle around in this huge house. We've been here so long, sometimes we forget we don't own the place. Until we remember how much money it takes to run it." She laughed in her easy, gentle way and smiled brightly. "It's so great to have you here."

"Thank you, Franny."

Christina led Dylan up the spiral staircase to a guest room. "Change into dry clothes. Meet me downstairs."

"Okay, Doc," Dylan said with a twinkle in his eye.

Christina wandered down the hall and pushed open her bedroom door. She needed a minute to collect herself.

Christina flopped onto the bed, covered her face with her hands and finally released the tears she had been holding back since she saw Dylan unconscious on the pavement of the school parking lot. Had she put him in harm's way? Had her accusations against Roger jeopardized those she cared about most?

Those she cared about most. The realization hit her hard, making her breath hitch in her throat.

That's why she had kept her mouth closed all those years. Roger would never atone for what he had done to her. And revealing the secret now had only hurt someone she had grown to care about.

It was too late to make Roger pay and now she had wakened a sleeping giant.

A fist of panic tightened in her chest.

Christina dug her fingers through her hair. She wanted nothing more than to bury herself in her work at the clinic. Forget about all the bad events swirling around in her personal life.

Just like she always had.

Christina stood and went into the adjoining bathroom. Between the tears and the rain, she had definitely seen better days. She leaned toward the mirror and ran a gentle finger over the dark smudges under her eyes. Maybe she'd get a better night's sleep here in her old bed without worrying about someone crawling through the window of her little cottage out in the woods. Or having her niece wake her up.

Then she remembered she wouldn't be getting much sleep tonight. Her job was to make sure Dylan was okay. And that made her feel really, really tired.

Christina dragged a brush through her hair and grimaced as it tugged through knots. Maybe Naomi, at least would have a good night's sleep tonight. Christina had been relieved to deliver the news that her young Amish friend was not pregnant.

After receiving the good news, Naomi and Christina had had a little chat. The Amish woman had had a relationship with Aaron Webb, a young man at one of the wealthy homes where she cleaned. During her running-around days, she had become friends with several townies, including Cheryl. Naomi had been alone with the young man at the home she cleaned and she feared she had gotten pregnant. However, after a long, frank discussion with Naomi, Christina discovered that the young woman couldn't have been pregnant. Her insular life had led to misinformation about the basics about the birds and the bees. One of which was what it took to become pregnant.

Naomi regretted going against her upbringing and the stress, no doubt, led to a disruption in her cycle. Poor sweet Naomi was repentant and maybe now she could get back on the right path.

Christina put the brush down and stared into the mirror, wondering if she'd ever find more to life than her work at the clinic. She quickly dismissed the thought and gave gratitude where gratitude was due.

Thank You, Lord. Naomi needed this second chance.

She hoped Naomi would take full advantage of her reprieve to live the life she aspired to. She had left the clinic with Cheryl, vowing she was going to go to the bishop and ask to start baptismal classes the first chance she got. Christina also suspected the young Amish woman would have to distance herself from her English friend, at least for now, possibly forever, to prove to the church leaders that she was committed to the Amish Way.

A knock sounded on her door and Christina rushed out of the bathroom to hear Franny's voice on the other side of her closed bedroom door. "Hello, Christina?"

Christina opened the door and smiled. "Hi, Franny."

"Sorry to bother you."

"It's fine. I hate to impose on you and Henry."

"I'm glad you did." Franny fiddled with the Precious Moments figurines on Christina's dresser. Christina's mother had purchased one for every occasion for her daughter. Many of them were delivered with flowers and a bouquet of balloons when her parents were out of town with a promise to *really* celebrate when they returned from a far-flung location. Christina always looked at them with a mix of love and nostalgia. She would rather have had her mom, not possessions.

But her parents were called to live a different kind of life, creating business start-ups and serving the less fortunate with their vast wealth. Parenting was low on their priority list. They made sure she and her siblings had a beautiful home, a solid education and loving caretakers, but they themselves were never present. Christina realized it could have been far worse. She had many blessings to be thankful for.

"Henry is going to the grocery store. We're wondering if there's anything you'd like?"

Christina smiled. "It really is good to be home." She leaned over and brushed a kiss across her former caretaker's cheek.

The older woman stepped back, tears glistening in her eyes. "Nice to have you home."

Dylan leaned back on the couch and lifted his feet up onto the ottoman. He tried not to wince as his head throbbed with the effort. It was late, very late, but Christina had insisted they sit up so she could monitor his concussion. He didn't want to give her any more reasons to fuss over him.

The fire crackled in the fireplace. The one thing that would have made the room more cozy was Christina sitting next to him and not over in the leather chair closer to the fireplace.

"When's the last time you sat and watched the fire?" he asked, smiling at Christina.

She smiled back and blinked slowly. "Life's been busy."

"It's amazing how the years roll by."

Christina arched an eyebrow. "Waxing poetic after hitting your head?"

"I have a softer side. I don't always show it." His sarcastic tone suggested otherwise, he feared. Sometimes he had a difficult time shutting it off.

Christina made a sound, suggesting she was giving it some thought. He wondered what she had concluded.

"You know, when we met in college, I knew you came from money, but I never imagined all this. You're loaded."

"My parents are loaded." Christina shrugged. "They have been very generous by paying for my education and supporting the healthcare clinic, but they made it clear when we were a young age that we could not ride on their coattails."

"You did them proud." Dylan stifled a yawn. What he wouldn't give to catch some sleep right now, especially after the fantastic dinner Franny had made.

Pink brightened her cheeks under the glow of the fireplace. She waved him off, unable to take the compliment.

"How come you never brought me home to meet your parents?" he asked, eager to keep the conversation going.

"I suppose we didn't date long enough for me to bring

you home to meet them. That would have meant things were getting serious."

"Fair enough," he whispered, feeling the jab like a knife to the heart. "Fair enough." He pulled his feet off the ottoman, rested his elbows on his thighs and leaned toward her. She was still far away from him across the room. "Have you ever brought a boyfriend home?"

Christina eyed him but she didn't seem mad, she seemed amused, curious. "You're chatty tonight."

He rubbed a hand across his face. "Well, if you insist on keeping me up, we might as well talk about something." He studied her carefully. "You didn't answer my question."

She shook her head. "I didn't realize we were playing truth or dare. I'll take a dare, then."

"A dare, huh?" He turned his attention back toward the cracking fire. "I suppose it's too late for games." He blinked his eyes slowly. They felt gritty from lack of sleep.

He watched as Christina leaned back in the leather chair and closed her eyes. He knew enough not to tell her she looked tired, but she did. The recent events had weighed heavily on her.

"When do you have to be back on campus for summer session?" Her question surprised him because she hadn't opened her eyes.

"Not for another week," he said. "I'm glad I've been available to help you out."

She opened her eyes and slowly turned her head toward him. "I appreciate it. And I'm grateful Georgia's been able to manage the clinic. I've never been away from work this much." She laughed, a tired sound. "She'll be looking for a raise."

"Being away from the clinic is a big change for you."

"Sometimes other things come up." There was a fatalistic quality to her voice.

"Ah, and now I'm your job."

"If that's what you want to call it." Her tone was hard to read.

Eager to change the subject, Dylan asked, "Did I detect a slight Pennsylvania Dutch accent in Henry and Franny? Well, not so much an accent, but in some of the expressions they use."

Christina laughed. "Nothing gets by you. Yes, Franny and Henry jumped the fence, as they say. My parents hired them on full-time to help them make the transition. They've been here ever since."

"Interesting."

Christina turned to Dylan. "How's your head?"

"Hard as a rock."

She gave him a skeptical glare.

"And your arm?"

He stretched out one, then the other. The pain from earlier had subsided. "Arms are good." He watched her intently, expecting her to contradict him.

"Good." She pulled her legs up into a crisscross position in the leather chair. "Now what should we talk about?"

"I'm out of ideas."

A quiet, tired laugh escaped her pink lips.

His chest grew tight with guilt. Christina was already exhausted and, because of him, she wasn't going to get much sleep while keeping an eye on him because of his concussion.

TEN

"Christina, Christina!" Franny's voice broke through Christina's fragmented dream. She bolted upright and blinked her tired eyes, struggling to focus on the dying embers in the fireplace. A rustling sound drew her attention to Dylan sprawled out on the leather couch.

Christina muttered, "My neck." Sleeping sitting up was no picnic. Tilting her head back and forth to ease out the kinks, she stared up at Franny, who was standing in front of her in her white bathrobe wringing her hands.

"I'm sorry to disturb you, Christina, but you'll want to see this."

Panic washed over Christina at Franny's frantic expression. The older woman was a rock, she didn't fluster easily. "What is it?" Christina glanced over at Dylan who had shifted into a seated position, his hair tousled from sleep. She was relieved he was alert and hadn't deteriorated as a result of his concussion.

Keenly aware of Franny standing in front of her wringing her hands, Christina walked over to Dylan. "How are you feeling?"

He furrowed his forehead and scrubbed a hand across his face. He had sleep lines on his cheek that touched her heart in an unexpected way. It made him look more vulnerable than she had ever seen him before, including after his accident yesterday.

"I've been better and I've been worse." He tapped his head. "Told you I had a hard head."

Christina nodded. "You should be out of the woods."

"Dr. Christina," Franny said, glancing repeatedly toward the kitchen, "You really need to see this."

Unease threaded its way up her spine. "I'll be right back," she said to Dylan.

She followed Franny into the kitchen. A small drop-down TV was mounted underneath the white cabinets. A commercial with a man dressed as the sun played on the small screen.

With a fluttering in her stomach, Christina turned to Franny. "What is it?"

Franny grabbed the remote and hit the rewind button. Out of the corner of Christina's eye, she noticed Dylan entering the room, his clothes rumpled. She didn't dare look down at her own.

"What's going on?" he asked, his voice gruff at this early hour. He ran a hand through his hair and tufts stood up at awkward angles. Dylan seemed too distracted to notice. Under other circumstances, Christina would have giggled, but the intense expression on Franny's face had a sobering effect.

Dylan pointed to the small screen and Christina refocused her attention. Even looking at the distorted image in rewind, she recognized the imposing figure.

Her world slowed and her mouth went dry.

Franny, still pointing the remote at the screen, rewound to a certain point, then hit Play.

Christina squinted at the small screen and stepped closer.

A camera crew was set up in front of Apple Creek High School. A petite woman with a microphone in her hand was saying, "Sources close to the school report that Roger Everett, the new coach of the Apple Creek High School girls' softball team and a member of the town council allegedly has engaged in inappropriate conduct with a young woman. We can't confirm if the conduct was with a current student or a former student or someone in the community. We have a call in to Principal Acer who has yet to return our calls."

The shot returned to the studio where a couple of newscasters started in on some happy chat. Christina swung around to face Dylan. "How did they find out?"

"Small town. Someone probably started doing some digging after my near miss yesterday."

"Do you think they know I was the one who accused Roger Everett?"

"Tough to say, but someone alerted the news less than twenty-four hours after you went to the principal."

Christina pulled out a stool at the island counter, its legs scraping against the hardwood floor. She planted her elbows on the cold granite countertop and dug her fingers through her hair. "I can't believe this."

Dylan sat down on the stool next to hers. "Maybe it's meant to unfold this way."

"I wanted to handle this discreetly. Roger has a wife and son…" She ran a finger across her chin. "I don't want them to have to endure a public lashing."

Roger's wife and son were innocent in all this.

Christina covered her mouth and closed her eyes. She didn't know where to go from here.

"This has to do with the near misses you mentioned last night?" Franny asked. "What did he do? You're scaring me."

Christina stood and touched Franny's arm. "Maybe you should sit down."

Franny shook her head. "I don't want to sit down. Tell me."

With a heavy heart, Christina shared her story of being attacked by Roger when she was in college and how, now, they suspected Roger might be coming after them to keep them quiet."

"Why now?" Franny's voice shook.

Dylan drew closer and rested his palm on the island. "An Amish girl was drugged on Roger's property. Christina treated the young woman at the clinic."

Franny gasped. "Did Roger attack her?"

"A Good Samaritan brought her to the clinic before whoever drugged her had a chance to assault her." Christina drew in a deep breath, then let it out. "There's no proof that it was Roger, but after I confronted him about attacking me, someone broke into my house, Dylan was nearly run over..." She let her voice trail off. She figured Franny had heard enough. "It's as if he's trying to prevent me from revealing his secret."

"Call Nick. Roger needs to be arrested. Now." Franny hustled over and snatched the phone from the base. *"Call him now."*

"Nick is aware of the situation. But as of now, Roger's been very careful. There's nothing to arrest him on."

Franny pressed her fingers to her cheeks. "This is horrible. Just horrible."

"If it makes you feel better, I'll touch base with Nick this morning just to make sure he saw the news." Christina wrapped her arm around the woman who had pretty much raised her. "It's okay. I'm safe. And soon Roger will mess up and he'll be arrested."

Christina just prayed no one was hurt before then.

Shortly after eating breakfast, Christina called into the clinic to check on Georgia, then Dylan and she decided to get some fresh air in the orchard behind the estate.

The blossoms had come and gone, and the first signs of fruit—apples and pears—were forming on the branches of the trees in the orchard surrounding the property. Dark clouds gathered in the distance. Christina had grabbed an umbrella—this time a black one with a hooked handle from the umbrella holder in the front hallway. Dylan had grabbed his gun and tucked it into his shoulder holster, concealing it under a light jacket.

Dylan and Christina carefully picked their steps around the muddy patches on the ground.

"I can't tell you how often I wandered around in these orchards. I made some big decisions out here." Christina lifted her face to the morning sun, her long brown hair flowing down her back.

"It's beautiful out here. I grew up in the city. The most trees I saw growing up were the ones the city planted in front of our yard, and every few years they died and had to be replanted. I always figured that was just a way of keeping the city workers employed."

Christina laughed, an infectious sound, a sound he had missed. "You have a warped way of looking at things."

"Realistic." He stuffed his hands in his front jeans pockets and took a wide step to miss a mud puddle.

"Okay, Mr. Realistic, what do you think is going on

here? Who do you think told the news we were up at the school?"

"Someone knew we were there. Someone tried to run me over in the school parking lot."

"I was hoping it was a kid with a newly minted driver's license who was afraid of getting a ticket. That's why he didn't stop after making you dive out of the way." The edge of sarcasm in her voice wasn't lost on him.

"Someone knew we were there."

"And they thought they were gunning for me since you had my floral umbrella."

Dylan nodded, not liking the sound of her theory, but he knew it had to be true.

"This has gotten out of control."

Seeing the worry on her face, he stepped closer. "I won't let anything happen to you."

"I'm not your problem."

"I don't consider you a problem." He couldn't keep the hurt from his voice.

Something flashed in her eyes that he couldn't quite read. The sudden need to confess, to tell her his true feelings swept over him. A realization that had solidified over the past few days.

"One of the biggest mistakes I ever made was letting you go."

Christina tipped her head and studied him. "God had a plan. I don't think we were meant to be together then. You were meant to be an FBI agent and I was meant to focus on my medical career." She smiled sadly. "Besides, we were babies back then. We didn't know what love was."

Dylan took a step closer. But maybe now they were meant to be together. He brushed his knuckles across her cheek. His heart started racing when she didn't back away.

"I've missed you," he whispered.

She looked away briefly, then lifted her eyes to his and cupped his cheek with the palm of her hand. Her lips curved into a small smile. He took this as an invitation. An invitation he had long been waiting for. He leaned forward and brushed his mouth against her warm lips, then lingered.

She smelled the same, tasted the same, felt the same.

A rustling in the nearby orchard had him pulling away. He glanced around but all he saw were trees. Acres and acres of trees.

"We probably shouldn't have done that." The smile in her eyes told him she was kidding.

He laughed. "I disagree. Now don't go overanalyzing everything."

"I haven't gotten where I am today without carefully considering my actions." Dylan smiled as Christina's cheeks grew red.

"Maybe *this* is God's plan." He knew it wasn't fair of him to use her words against her and he still wasn't one hundred percent sure where he stood with this whole God thing. He hadn't grown up in the faith until his mother died and mostly he was only mildly interested in Christina's devotion to her faith. It's obvious it had given her focus, contentment, a direction.

He shook away the thought. One mystery to solve at a time.

Christina took a step and stumbled. "Oh, my shoe is untied." She bent over to tie it and something zinged over her head. Dylan spun around to see an arrow sticking out of a tree.

Christina straightened, her eyes wide with shock when

she noticed the arrow. Dylan lunged forward, took her under his arm and moved her toward the house.

"Go! Go! Go!"

ELEVEN

Christina's chest heaved as she struggled to catch her breath when they reached the safety of her childhood home. Dylan slammed the French doors closed and turned the lock.

"What was that all about? Did someone try to hit us with an arrow?" She couldn't process what had happened. "Does Roger even know how to do that?" Her mind's eye traveled back to the targets set up outside the barn in the back of the Everett's home.

"Stay here. I'm going to go out there and see if I can track the person down."

Christina grabbed Dylan's arm. "No, let's call the sheriff's office. Roger has to be out of his mind if he's out there with a bow and arrow. *Please*, stay put. You need rest after your concussion."

Dylan glanced toward the locked French door and the orchard beyond. He ran his hand over the back of his neck. "The only hope we have of catching Roger—or whoever it is—is if I go out there now."

"But—"

Dylan tipped his head in her direction. "I've been trained by the FBI, remember? I can handle myself."

"You're not going to be dissuaded?" Her tone was laced with hope and fear.

Dylan turned the bolt on the French door. "Lock up behind me," he said, ignoring her plea to wait for the sheriff or one of his deputies. "Go ahead and call the sheriff. Tell them the shot came from the southwest corner of the orchard."

With that, Dylan turned and headed out the door with his gun at the ready. For some reason the fact that he was carrying caught her off guard.

The reality of that made her sadder than it should have. He was meant to be an FBI agent. He would go back to being one when his leave was over. And her life was here in Apple Creek at the clinic.

She touched her lips, thinking about his gentle kiss, and a hollowness expanded inside her.

It all circled around again to the reasons they couldn't be together, not the least of which was her most immediate concern. Someone was out to get her.

All indications pointed to Roger Everett.

Christina bolted the door and tracked Dylan's movements across the thick sloping grass until he disappeared into the orchard.

Please keep Dylan safe...

The memory of the arrow zinging over her head made her nerves hum with anxiety. A strange sense of being watched made the fine hairs on the back of her neck stand on edge. She moved to one side of the French doors so that she'd be out of sight.

Then, snapping out of it, she ran to get her smartphone from the kitchen island. She called her brother's number directly. After she told him about their emergency, she hung up.

Panic and a lack of patience surged through her as she pinched the bridge of her nose and squeezed her eyes shut.

"What's wrong now?"

Christina startled at Franny's voice. She was standing only a few feet away.

Christina's hand flew to her throat and she let out a tiny squeak. "Oh, you scared me."

Franny rocked back. "Is it Roger again?"

"It could be." *It has to be.* Christina tried to shake her nerves. "Dylan and I were taking a walk in the orchard and someone shot an arrow near us."

Franny pursed her lips. "An arrow?"

"Do you know anyone around here or on the neighboring properties who practices archery?" Even as she asked the question, her memory flitted back to the day she walked toward the Everetts' barn with Roger stalking behind her. Targets had been tacked to hay bales.

"You know as well as I do that your parents own acres and acres. No one else should be around. Not for quite a distance." Franny moved in front of the French doors and squinted, not able to see anything out of the ordinary. "I can have Henry look around. He's been tinkering in the basement workshop all morning."

"It might not be safe. Dylan's out there now searching for the person. I called Nick, too."

"Good, good," Franny said, assuming everything had been settled since Christina had called her brother, the deputy. "He'll get to the bottom of this."

Christina let out a long sigh. "Everything has gotten out of control. I haven't handled this well at all." Maybe she should have held her accusations close to the vest. Maybe they shouldn't have gone to the school.

How could they *not* have gone to the school?

Now everyone was on the defensive.

Now, after the way she had handled things, Roger was stirring the pot.

And coming after her and those she cared about.

Did she care about Dylan?

The realization pierced her heart like the arrow that had pierced the bark inches from where she had stood in the orchard.

She couldn't deal with that thought. Not now.

Christina feared the price one had to pay for revealing the truth might not be worth it.

Her life and the lives of those she cared deeply about were at risk.

Franny paced the kitchen, not used to all the commotion. "I don't think Christina should go back to the clinic. She should hunker down—"

"Um, guys, I'm right here. I'm a big girl," Christina said, mostly because she hated when people talked about her as if she weren't there but partly because she liked her independence. She didn't want anyone to steal that from her.

But day by day, incident by incident, someone *was* stealing it from her. And if they couldn't find evidence, it would continue.

Roger would continue.

"Whoever's harassing you isn't fooling around," Nick said, in the way older brothers tended to talk to little sisters. Christina resented that, too. Inwardly she shook her head. She was in one grumpy mood and none of this was helping.

"Whoever? Don't you mean Roger Everett?" He was

the only one who made sense. She threatened his future, so he was going to ruin hers.

"Right now, we have no evidence tying Roger to the assaults and harassment," Nick said. "But based on information you gave us, he's our best lead."

"Any word after checking the kids' phones from the accident at school? They video everything," Christina said.

"We're still running through it, but nothing new. No one captured the car that nearly ran Dylan over."

Dylan watched Christina, his expression unreadable. Her brother's pointing out that there was no real evidence against Roger and Dylan's silence seemed to bring back all sorts of feelings of insecurity and pain.

Was I responsible for the attack? Am I to blame?

She refused to go back there.

Christina clenched her fists. "Who else would be coming after me? I finally revealed Roger's dirty little secret and now he's angry. He's doing everything he can to silence me."

Nick slouched on the stool. He pushed his hand through his hair, mussing it. He looked at her. "I don't doubt your story for a minute…about what he tried to do to you when you were in college. What I'm struggling to grasp is that he'd gain by going after you now." Nick cleared his throat. "He got away with it. Why stir things up?"

Christina slid off the stool and went over to the fridge and grabbed a bottle of water. "Because he's afraid I'll no longer remain silent. Because maybe this is bigger than me. What if he had attempted to attack the young Amish girl on his property?" She locked gazes with Dylan. "We have to stop him."

"What happened when you called Roger this morning?" Dylan asked.

"Yeah, I reached Linda about an hour ago. I think I woke her up. She sounded tired." Nick's tone was strained. "Linda's not doing well."

"That's what makes this so hard. She doesn't need this stress. It's not good for her." Christina set her bottle of water on the island and rested her hip against the edge of the counter. She tapped her fingers on the granite.

"Was Roger with Linda?" She found herself holding her breath, waiting for the answer. If Roger was with Linda, what did that say about the arrow that almost pierced her head? Could he have gotten home before Linda missed him?

"Linda said Roger was tied up with some city council stuff."

"Had she or Roger seen the news?"

"Yes, she said it was all lies. She said the truth would come out."

"What does that mean?" Christina asked.

"Linda wouldn't elaborate." Nick shook his head in disbelief. "When I pressed for more information, she said she wasn't feeling well and ended the call." The stress was evident in the lines around her brother's mouth and warm eyes. "I'm stuck between a rock and a hard place, here. Roger's been my friend for years." He shook his head in despair and disbelief. "Linda's had a rough go of it health-wise. Roger and she have had their differences in the past, but I thought they had worked things out."

Christina approached her brother and placed her hand on his back. "I never wanted you to know," she whispered, feeling Dylan's eyes on her from across the kitchen island. "You and Roger were like brothers." She tilted her head and mustered a smile.

"You shouldn't have kept that secret. I feel horrible that he hurt you." Nick leaned back and took her hand in his. "I thank God every day that he didn't hurt you worse. But he needs to be punished for what he did to you. And if he hurt anyone else."

"I fear there's no evidence from back then, but he's so reckless now. We'll catch him." Christina squeezed her brother's hand in a show of confidence. "Listen, no more blaming one another. Roger's the one who deserves the blame. Let's find a way to get him." She left out the part about getting him before he got her.

Something on the television caught Christina's eye. She moved closer and turned up the sound. There, standing in front of the town hall on Main Street, were Roger and Linda Everett.

"Linda must be feeling better." The old song, "Stand By Your Man," floated through Christina's brain. Something about a woman having to put up with a man's garbage just because she was unfortunate enough to have picked a loser always unnerved her.

No wonder Christina was still single.

Her eyes were locked on Linda on the TV screen. Better single than to be hitched to a man like Roger Everett. Something niggled at her. Maybe Linda had realized that. When she'd first met the woman, she seemed to be distant from Roger and talked about their marriage in the past tense.

Maybe they could use that...

Since Christina was lost in thought, it took a moment for Roger's words coming from the TV's speakers to seep into her brain. He yelled them, more than spoke them.

"It pains me to come forward," he said, the *P* sounding like a sharp puff of air in the reporter's mike that Roger grabbed and pulled closer to his mouth. "I've been a friend, serving two tours of duty, with her brother, Sheriff's Deputy, Nick Jennings, who I'm sure will be just as hurt by this discovery."

Sweat trickled down Christina's back as she drew closer to the TV screen. Her frustration grew as Roger, basking in the attention, kept talking around his point. "…I'm sure many people are appreciative of the free healthcare clinic…" The walls of the room grew close.

What is Roger talking about?

She didn't dare verbalize her question for fear she'd miss what Roger had to say.

"My wife went into the clinic recently…"

Christina's pulse whooshed in her ears.

"…and Dr. Christina Jennings offered her pain medication. With the condition that she fill the prescription, then give back some of the meds to Dr. Jennings."

"What are you suggesting?" the reporter asked.

"Dr. Christina Jennings is dealing pharmaceuticals. What else would she be doing with the extra pills?"

Christina's heart sunk. "What? No, no, no…"

"Needless to say, my wife wanted nothing to do with this. There's an epidemic of unscrupulous doctors illegally prescribing controlled substances and unfortunately, Apple Creek is not immune. I wouldn't doubt if we found out her clinic is providing these drugs to our young people."

A hot and cold sweat washed over Christina. "He's lying," she whispered. "He's lying."

"Dr. Christina Jennings is an unethical doctor. And

until people like my wife and I are brave enough to stand up to such misdeeds, they will continue."

The pretty reporter smiled awkwardly into the camera. "Do your accusations have anything to do with the allegations that you've had inappropriate contact with young women? Some students place Christina Jennings at the high school prior to those reports being made public. Was she the person who accused you of inappropriate conduct with young women?"

Roger gave her a stiff smile. Linda was off camera. "That's the thing. Those accusations against me were made because I vowed to fight this drug problem head-on. Dr. Jennings threatened to cause trouble for me, but this is too big an issue for me to be bullied into silence."

The walls heaved and Christina swayed. Dylan put his hand on the small of her back. "Sit down." Dylan tried to guide her away from the TV to a nearby stool.

Christina stepped away from his touch, anger, frustration, disbelief tangled inside her. "I'm *not* going to sit." She jabbed her finger at the TV screen while the newscasters went on to report on something else, the weather, the high school sports team, whatever. She couldn't think straight.

She spun around to face Dylan. "Roger Everett's lying. And I need your help to prove it."

TWELVE

Dylan tried to guide Christina to a chair with a gentle touch to the small of her back. During the brief moment before she brushed him off, he could feel the subtle tremble coursing through her.

Roger Everett was backed into a corner and had come out swinging. His blow had struck Christina square on the jaw, sending her reeling.

Dylan turned off the television and Christina stood staring at the blank screen. "I can't believe Roger accused me of pushing painkillers. Of being unethical."

Nick exhaled between tight lips, his frustration evident. "I had always considered myself a good judge of character. This guy—" he shook his head, the rage rolling off him "—Roger and I were the best of friends. We served in the army together."

Dylan watched Christina, ready to catch her as she swayed on her feet. She finally sat on a stool and leaned forward, folding her arms around her middle. He wanted to wrap his arm around her, comfort her, but the invisible wall she had erected left him feeling helpless and angry.

Christina had accused Roger of inappropriate behavior and now he was going to do everything he could to push back.

"This stops here. I'm going to talk to Roger and his wife. You stay here with my sister." Nick pulled out his car keys.

Christina looked up, a weary expression in her eyes. "What are you going to do? What are you going to say?" Her voice was barely a whisper.

Nick sat next to her and put his hand on her back. She leaned into him briefly, then sat up straight. "I'm going to talk to Roger. I'm going to treat him as I would any other person who made an accusation. I have to separate my job from my personal life. I have to hear what he and Linda have to say."

Christina swiped away a tear that slid down her cheek. "But you don't…" Dylan suspected she was going to say, *You don't believe him*, but something stopped her. The pained expression on her face tore at Dylan's heart. Even if he hadn't known Christina, truly known the type of person she was, the type of physician she was, the hurt in her eyes would make any observant person with any amount of compassion realize she had been falsely accused.

Nick stood up. "I don't believe for a minute that you've done anything unethical or illegal. But I have to approach this situation objectively. Try to defuse it." He put his hat on. "Clear your name."

Dylan crossed his arms. "Roger Everett is trying to muddy the waters after we reported him to the principal. He figures if he turns public opinion against you, people might forget to look at him."

Christina dragged a hand through her hair. "He's delusional. Principal Acer can't ignore our claims even if he does try to turn the blame around."

"No, but he might create enough diversion so people think you're lying. Looking to retaliate," Nick said. "This gives people a reason to not believe you." Nick's phone rang and he grabbed it off his duty belt. After a minute, he hung up. "I have to go." He strode toward the door, then turned around. "You know how to reach me." Then he lowered his voice and smiled at his sister. "It's going to be okay."

"Listen to your brother. It is going to be okay," Dylan said.

Christina shook her head. "People won't believe him, will they?"

Dylan patted her knee platonically. "Roger's a desperate man. Basically, he had to respond in some way. His accusation against you will confuse people."

Christina exhaled sharply. "These accusations could ruin my career. Destroy the clinic, especially after the recent incidences of young people being drugged at parties. The residents of Apple Creek won't look kindly on anyone who they think may have contributed to the downfall of the youth in this community."

"*Have* you contributed to the downfall of the youth in Apple Creek?"

Christina snapped her head around to look at him, anger coming off of her in waves. "Of course not. But we have to figure out who stole the drugs from the clinic. That won't help my case."

"Stop automatically thinking the worst." Dylan flattened a hand to his chest. "Have you forgotten I'm a lawyer?"

Christina laughed, a sound devoid of humor. "Have

you ever practiced law?" She shook her head again and glanced toward the television screen, no doubt Roger's accusations replaying through her head.

"Um, I worked for a few months doing real estate transactions until I was admitted to the FBI Academy."

"Great." She rolled her eyes and smiled, this time genuinely.

"I'm a smart guy. The first thing we'll do is hit Roger Everett with a slander suit. A person can't publicly accuse someone. And he does not have the truth on his side."

"This is all crazy, but I don't think we should react yet. I'm afraid a lawsuit will fuel the fire." She rubbed her temples. "I have to think."

Christina took a sip of her tea, letting the warm liquid slide down her throat. Franny had always offered her tea and a cookie when something had gone wrong at school or when the mean girls had been especially mean or when her heart had been broken.

Christina had consumed a lot of tea and cookies when this man sitting next to her had broken her heart.

After her nerves settled, she put down the cup on the saucer. In the other room she could hear Franny running the water and loading the dishwasher. She hadn't realized until now how such mundane household sounds could be so comforting. Why had she stayed away from this place for so long? Perhaps it was a mix of yearning and nostalgia. She longed for a different childhood, with a mom who stayed home and baked cookies, but instead she had been given a driven mother and father who traveled the globe building an empire, but who always gave back with generous hearts. And her parents had ensured that she and her siblings had a loving influence at home.

Christina shifted to look at Dylan, anxiety bubbling up inside her. "I'm at a loss. I usually bury myself in work when I'm stressed." She pushed to her feet and adjusted her shirt over her waistband.

Dylan stood and looked down at her. "I'm sorry. It's tough." He rubbed the back of his neck. "We'll get to the bottom of this."

"I'm not going to let that…let that…" She struggled to tone down her anger and think of an appropriate and suitable word to describe the man who had once again hijacked her life. She had regained control of the reins before. She'd do it again.

Roger Everett would not win.

Christina strode across the room and grabbed her purse from the foyer table. "It was a mistake to close the clinic for the day. It's not fair. He's not going to keep me away from my job." Her mind raced. She couldn't think clearly. "It sends the wrong message."

"Wait. It's only for the day. Georgia's been working long hours. She needs a break, too. If someone has an emergency, they can go to the hospital."

"But…" A million reasons it would be preferable for patients to come to the clinic instead of the ER ran through her head, cost being part of the equation. She was so tired she couldn't articulate the words.

"You can't do everything. We'll take each day as it comes." Something in Dylan's tone made her stop and turn slowly on her heel. Franny walked into the room, paused, apparently assessing the thick tension hanging in the air, then muttered something and disappeared back into the kitchen.

Christina set her purse down and walked slowly toward Dylan. "I have to go. It's who I am." Her heart beat loudly in her ears. It felt like one of those moments when she was about to hear something she didn't want to hear, learn something she could never unlearn.

"I don't want anything to happen to you." Dylan stood as if rooted to his spot. "I wouldn't forgive myself." The pain that flashed across his face broke her heart.

She took a step closer to him but something kept her from reaching out, from touching his arm. "Believe it or not, I'm a grown woman. I've managed to make it this far on my own."

They stared into each other's eyes momentarily. She was the first to break contact. "There's no reason you should feel so…" She didn't know the word she was looking for. Controlling? Possessive? Territorial? But all those words had such negative connotations and she felt in her bones that Dylan's actions stemmed from a place of love.

Love. She let that thought sink in.

She closed her eyes briefly, trying to settle her conflicting emotions. Did Dylan care for her that deeply? She couldn't get sucked in. She'd be crushed when he decided to go back to the FBI.

Dylan shifted his feet and rubbed his hand across his stubbled jaw. "You're right. I push too hard sometimes. It's my need for control, I guess." He smiled—a sad smile.

"That's what makes you a good agent," she said, confident that he must have been a great FBI agent. "It's the reason you'll eventually go back." She knew in her heart that it was just a matter of time before he went back.

"I should have been a better agent." Dylan stared off in the middle distance.

Christina tucked her hands into her pockets, trying to keep from fidgeting as she waited for the man she once loved, the man she once thought she had a future with, to continue.

"My partner, Special Agent Reed, died in the line of duty because of me." His voice grew quiet. "It was my job to show her the ropes, to protect her. But I sent her to talk to a confidential informant alone and she was murdered in cold blood." His voice was oddly steady, as if he had been over the story a million times in his head. And beaten himself up over it with every rehashing.

"Agent Reed was killed doing her job. You can't take the blame."

"I was the senior agent. I should have kept her safe."

"Like you're supposed to keep me safe?"

Dylan tipped his head, but didn't say anything.

"Why did you come to Apple Creek?" Christina's chest tightened. How had she gotten the nerve to ask him the very question she'd wondered about from the first day she realized he was in Apple Creek? The first time her heart rate had quickened when she recognized his broad shoulders, the familiar way he rubbed the back of his neck, his penchant for apple pie and ice cream, never to be called à la mode.

"I came to Apple Creek because I had connections with the university. I wanted to return to a time when I still had hope for the future. A time when I thought I could do anything." Her heart shattered in a million pieces for him. She knew what it meant to be broken. "And I'd be lying if I didn't say that I came back for you."

The steady strum of her heart beating in her ears made her dizzy. She pressed her lips together and smiled. She leaned forward and brushed a kiss across his cheek.

Christina pulled back and Dylan watched her expectantly.

"Dylan, you are a good man. But I am not the woman I was when we met in college. And I cannot fix the hurt inside you. I don't have it in me. You have to find a way to do that yourself." She shrugged as she took a step backward. "You see, I'm already busy trying to fix me. And God knows, I'm a work in progress. You have to find healing inside *you*."

Dylan rubbed the unshaven stubble on his jaw. "It's been a long few days for everyone. I respect that. But please, allow me to keep you safe while I am here. Roger's too much of a loose cannon to let our differences put you in danger."

She studied him for a long moment and lifted her hand to cup his cheek. "I'll be fine."

Christina had only recently come to terms with her past. Only recently admitted to those whom she loved that she had been attacked. She wasn't ready to open her heart.

She first had to put together the pieces of her life. A life that was imploding at this very moment.

But she couldn't be foolish. She had to stay safe.

Christina strode toward the door and scooped up her purse. She turned around when she reached the door. "You coming?"

Half of Dylan's mouth quirked into a grin. "I told you I was a good lawyer."

Christina cocked her head. "How's that?"

"I crushed in debate class."

Christina laughed, feeling the weight of the absolutely crummy day lifting. "Was Bodyguard 101 one of the classes you excelled in?"

Dylan opened the door for Christina and gave her a weary look. "Let's hope you never have to find out."

THIRTEEN

A sheriff's cruiser sitting in the healthcare clinic's parking lot was not totally unexpected. However, the sight of it made Dylan realize Christina wouldn't be able to go through any part of her day without a reminder of the events hanging over her head. Not that she would forget.

"I thought your brother was headed over to talk to Roger," Dylan said, as he slammed the gearshift into Park.

Christina pushed her door open. "That's not my brother's cruiser, it's his boss, Sheriff Maxwell," she said, sounding weary. "Maybe Nick's still tracking down Roger."

Dylan pushed his door open and canvassed the parking lot. Long shadows from the towering trees cloaked the far corners of the lot. "Come on." He moved in close to Christina and ushered her to the door, remembering the shock of the arrow vibrating in the tree near her head.

Christina looked up at him while they both quickened their pace toward the door.

"You really don't think Roger would try anything, do you? Not with the sheriff here." Her tone held an air of disbelief and frustration.

"He's desperate."

"Well, hopefully Nick tracked him down already."

She yanked open the door and came up short. "Hello, Sheriff Maxwell."

"Hello, Dr. Jennings." The sheriff stood up from the blue plastic chair and offered his hand to Christina.

The sheriff then turned to Dylan. "I don't believe we've met."

"Professor Dylan Hunter."

The sheriff seemed taken aback, then realization dawned. "Ah, you're the FBI agent that Nick said was keeping an eye on his sister."

"Something like that," Christina muttered. "But I like to think I can look after myself." She immediately regretted the edge to her tone. The sheriff was simply doing his job.

"Hello, Dr. Christina."

Christina's attention was drawn to Georgia, sitting across from the seat the sheriff had vacated, twisting her hands in her lap.

"Why are you here?" Christina asked, confusion clouding her brain. After everything going on this morning, Christina had told Georgia to close the clinic for the day.

Georgia opened her mouth to speak and the sheriff interrupted her. "I contacted Georgia to meet me here. Considering the allegations."

"Okay." Christina bowed her head and tucked a strand behind her ear. "You have to know I'm not pushing painkillers. No part of my practice is illegal."

"Listen, Christina, I'm not the enemy. I'm here to clear things up." The sheriff sat back down, leaned forward and rested his elbows on his knees. "Have a seat."

Christina sat down and Dylan moved toward the wall, leaning one shoulder against it.

"Drugs are a big issue in Apple Creek," the sheriff said. "It's important that I take the allegations Roger Everett made against you seriously."

"What are you suggesting?" Her face started to tingle and tiny dots danced in her line of vision.

"You know about a young woman who had been drugged on campus a few weeks ago?" The sheriff interrupted her thoughts.

Christina nodded, anxiety tightening its fist around her throat.

"She had been high on a drug that is normally prescribed for ethical reasons. I can't discount the fact that Roger's claiming your clinic was offering prescriptions by less than ethical means."

"He's lying." Christina sought assurance first from Dylan, then the sheriff. "Mrs. Everett is very ill. She needs pain medication. I only offered her a prescription after I consulted with her doctors in Buffalo."

"I've known you and your brother for a long time. I want you to tell me exactly what happened when Linda Everett came in."

"I'm bound by doctor–patient confidentiality. You know that."

The sheriff paused for a minute. "Are you prescribing prescription painkillers illegally?"

Dylan levered off the wall and crossed his arms over his chest. "You don't have to answer these questions."

"No, I want to. I've done nothing wrong," Christina said adamantly, heat firing in her cheeks. "I'm an ethical doctor. I keep the medicine cabinets locked. I know the dangers of drugs when taken inappropriately. But recently, I have learned some antianxiety meds went missing."

"Oh?" The sheriff let the single word hang out there. "Who has access?"

"Well, Georgia and I do. I trust Georgia completely."

"Thank you," Georgia said, continuing to nervously twist her hands in her lap.

"I find it hard to believe you'd do anything unethical," the sheriff said. "Let's focus on the missing drugs. Who else has access?"

The rustling of the door handle drew their attention. Dylan stepped forward, looking like he was ready to slam it shut again. He moved in front of the opening, blocking Christina's ability to see who was at the door.

After a brief moment, Dylan stepped aside and Cheryl and Naomi entered the clinic. Christina got to her feet, feeling a bit like she had been caught doing something wrong. She supposed that was how most people felt after they had been questioned by the sheriff.

"Can I help you, Naomi?" Christina asked.

Naomi took a step back, her long skirt fluttering around her boots. "I came to clean. I heard you were closed for the day."

Christina furrowed her brow, trying to dismiss the suspicion that seeped into her bones. It was Naomi's turn to look confused. "I called earlier to see when would be a good time to come in and Georgia told me."

Georgia nodded.

Naomi held out her hand. "Cheryl gave me a ride from the end of my road. I didn't want to deal with any grief from my parents."

Cheryl shrugged playfully. "We enjoy hanging out."

Naomi dragged her hand down the string on her bonnet. "Maybe after I'm baptized, my parents won't be as strict. They'll know I'm committed."

The sheriff stood and the two newcomers looked at him with suspicion. "Is something going on?" Cheryl asked, stuffing her hands in her pants pockets.

"Do you both have access to the clinic during off hours?"

Pink colored Naomi's cheeks. "I clean a lot when Dr. Christina's here, but sometimes I do it after she's closed the clinic."

"And you come with her?" The sheriff gave Cheryl a pointed glare.

"I hate to be here by myself, especially at night," Naomi said. "It's creepy."

Cheryl shifted her stance, a sense of unease pervading the small space. "Yep, I'm her taxi."

"Nothing else?" the sheriff asked.

"Like what?" Cheryl bit out, suddenly getting defensive.

"Gaining access to drugs or old prescription pads."

Cheryl jerked her head back and frowned. "Never. So not cool."

Goose bumps raced across Christina's skin. Something in the defiant expression of the young girl set off her internal alarm. And based on the hard set of Dylan's jaw, he had noticed it, too.

Cheryl jammed her fists under her armpits and a muscle worked in her jaw. "I'm not going to stand here while you accuse me of doing something I didn't do."

Dylan held up his hands, trying to defuse the situation. "No one is accusing you of anything. Take it easy."

Cheryl smacked his arm away. "Don't tell me to take

it easy." The young girl huffed and puffed and acted like a three-year-old having a temper tantrum.

She's protesting too much, Dylan thought.

Dylan had seen enough bad guys proclaiming their innocence to know Cheryl had done something wrong. He made eye contact with the sheriff.

"Cheryl, if you have something to share, you better do it now," the sheriff said. "We're going to find out sooner or later and we'll go easier on you if you cooperate."

Naomi turned toward her friend, the look of confusion and innocence in such contrast to the more worldly girl's surly expression. "Did you bring the drugs to the party?"

Cheryl spun to face Naomi. "No, I would never do that." She jerked her head back. "They're making things up. Don't you see that? Dr. Christina is afraid of losing her practice and now she's trying to pin it on me." Her voice grew shrill. "Adults never believe kids."

Christina stood, adjusting her shirt over the top of her jeans. "Cheryl, you have to tell the truth. My livelihood is on the line. The future of this clinic is on the line." She lifted her finger in a hold-on-a-minute gesture, then turned to Georgia. "Do you know where the lab reports are?"

"Yes, they're by the computer."

Christina retrieved them. "May I share this information, Naomi?" Christina leaned and whispered something to Naomi and then the young Amish girl nodded.

"The drug in Naomi's system after the barn party is consistent with the drugs that went missing from the clinic. Did you bring them, Cheryl?" Christina jabbed her finger at the piece of paper.

Cheryl wrapped her arms around herself, looking much younger and not as tough as she had a minute ago.

"I don't know why you're blaming me. I didn't do anything. I mean, why would I check on Naomi if I drugged her?" She twisted her face.

"I don't think you meant to hurt her, but whoever you gave or sold the drugs to dropped some in Naomi's drink. That scared you, so you came running to the clinic to check on her."

"I have no idea what you're talking about," Cheryl insisted.

"We're trying to get to the bottom of this," Dylan said, trying to appeal to the young woman. "The police will be looking at everyone who had access to the clinic."

"The more defensive you get, the closer we're going to scrutinize your activities," the sheriff added. "Tell us what's going on."

"Tell them," Naomi pleaded. "Someone drugged me. I could have been really hurt or worse." She visibly shuddered. "Do you want that to happen to someone else?"

"I have nothing to say." Cheryl yanked open the clinic door. She paused and turned to Naomi. "Get your own ride home. And don't call me anymore. You're nothing but trouble."

The clinic door slammed shut and all eyes moved to Naomi. She looked lost.

"Cheryl's been a good friend. I don't believe she'd steal drugs," Naomi said, her voice shaky. "I don't."

Sheriff Maxwell stood. "We'll look into it."

Naomi stood there with eyes wide. "It wonders me if I should come back another time."

"I think it would be best if you called it a day," the sheriff said.

Naomi nodded her bonneted head. Obviously sensing

her discomfort, Georgia stood and said, "If it's okay, I'll take Naomi home."

"That would be great," Christina said, offering her coworker a warm smile.

The two women slipped out the door. Christina looked more frightened than Dylan had ever seen her. She had almost been run over by a car, had her home broken into and an arrow missed her head, but her true fear stemmed from the realization that her healthcare clinic could be in jeopardy. If people found out the drugs had originated here, her license could be at stake.

Christina turned to the sheriff. "I have never done anything unethical or illegal when it comes to scripts. I'll cooperate fully."

The sheriff nodded.

"I'll see that she gets safely home," Dylan added. The two men shook hands.

The sheriff took a step toward the door, then paused. "I think it would be best if you came into the station to make a statement."

"A statement?" Christina ran her finger along her bottom lip.

"Yes. I understand Roger Everett attacked you when you were in high school."

"I have no proof." Her face flushed dark red. Dylan wanted to reassure her, but feared she might rebuff his offer of support.

"We've had a few other cases recently."

Christina's eyes grew wide.

"Roger wasn't on our radar for them, but once your brother told me about the incident between you and Roger, I did some investigating. He was in the area. If we can't get him for attacking you, maybe we can pin one of the more recent assaults on him."

Christina sat down slowly on one of the hard plastic chairs. "Oh, wow." She bowed her head, then lifted it. "What about the drugs stolen from my clinic?"

"I'm going to take a hard look at Cheryl. I also suggest you change the locks on the door and the medicine cabinets."

Chamomile tea did nothing to calm the sense of unease Christina felt as she sat in the dark of the early morning, staring out the French doors overlooking the orchard. Dylan had gotten up even earlier to run by his apartment and then go to an appointment in Buffalo with the FBI.

She couldn't believe the sheriff had Roger Everett in his sights for a few recent attacks. Sheriff Maxwell had said a young woman came forward after the news that Roger had ties with the girls' softball team. She had thwarted unwanted advances from Roger. She'd dismissed it, calling herself fortunate, but something about the intense look in his eyes unnerved her. The young woman didn't report the incident initially because she figured her parents, fearing for her safety, would make her move back home and she enjoyed living on campus. But, now, after seeing the news reports, she couldn't in good conscience remain quiet.

Christina should have never remained quiet. If she had reported Roger, how many women would she have spared? Guilt tightened its ruthless fist in her gut.

She pulled the tea bag out of her mug and dropped it on the saucer.

Abusers were often charismatic. They had a different public persona than they did in private. That's probably how Roger lured people into a sense of comfort. Maybe he had delusions that the women really liked him.

Christina took a long sip of her tea, feeling the hot liquid travel down her throat.

She hoped that through all of this, Linda could manage. Dealing with a serious disease was hard enough. Now this.

Bowing her head, she said a silent prayer. *Dear Lord, please watch over Linda Everett and give her strength in her time of illness. Bring her comfort.*

A thump at the window made her startle and look up. The first fingers of dawn stretched above the horizon. Her heart raced as her eyes scanned the back deck. A robin floundered on the deck, having flown into the window. Christina glanced down at the lock on the door. She had to go out and help the poor creature. She glanced over her shoulder. The rest of the house was sleeping.

Christina flipped the lock and was bending over to remove the rod bracing the door shut when she noticed the robin stretch its wings and fly away.

"Good job, little guy." She smiled, surprised by the relief she felt that the bird had only been stunned, yet angry with herself for being so afraid to go out on her deck because of all the recent events.

Her cell phone chirped, snapping her out of her scrambled thoughts. She glanced at the caller ID, but didn't recognize the number.

"Hello."

Silence stretched across the line.

"Hello?" she said again, this time louder.

"Dr. Christina…" The voice broke into sobs.

"Yes, this is Dr. Christina."

"I know it's early, but it's my mom." A male voice cracked.

Realization dawned. "Matthew Everett?"

He sniffed. "Yes, my mom isn't doing well. Can you help her?"

Christina pressed her lips together, hating that she was hesitant. "Matthew, your father won't want me to come. He's…" She let her words trail off. "Is your father there?"

"No, he went to Buffalo early for some meetings. I'm afraid he's going to be gone all day." Matthew's voice sounded stronger, yet still strained from the stress of his mother's illness.

"Did you call him?" Christina stared out the back window, watching the morning sky above the orchard growing brighter.

"Yes. He said he'd be back by dinner and that he checked on my mom before he left. I don't think he realized how bad she is. She's shaking." Christina could hear his ragged breathing over the line. "I think she's in horrible pain but won't take anything because my dad has made her afraid to take the pain medications. After that news conference and all." Christina couldn't pinpoint the emotion she sensed floating across the line.

She flattened her hand over her mouth, indecision capturing her voice. The house was quiet, save for the occasional sounds of settling. She had taken an oath. Memories of helping Nick's mother-in-law in her final days came to mind.

Despite everything swirling around, she had to help Linda. *She had to.* She wouldn't be able to live with herself if she didn't.

"What time is your dad coming home?" She glanced up at the clock. It was a few minutes before seven.

"He said he wouldn't be able to get home until at least four." She heard a muffled sound over the line. "Can you come? *Please*."

This information lined up with what Nick had told Christina yesterday after talking with Roger. He claimed he was innocent and was going to go about his business, which included a trip to Buffalo for business meetings. Roger was as adamant about his innocence as he was about Christina's guilt.

Now they were at a standstill until the sheriff's department uncovered evidence.

Christina drew in a deep breath.

"Yes, but don't tell your dad. Promise?" Christina said.

"I won't. Thank you." The relief was evident in Matthew's voice. "I'll leave the front door unlocked for you. Come right in and go to the bedroom at the top of the stairs. I'm afraid to leave my mom's side."

Christina glanced down at her PJ bottoms. "I'll be there in less than ten minutes."

FOURTEEN

Christina's brain knew that Roger Everett wasn't home, but someone needed to alert her body's involuntary response system. The flight part of her fight-or-flight response was waging a mighty battle. Yet she strode up the porch steps at the Everetts' home. Linda needed her.

If her personal code of ethics hadn't been so high, she wouldn't have responded to Matt's call at all. But how could she ignore Linda's suffering?

Christina pushed back her shoulders and knocked softly on the door, more as a formality. Matthew had told her to walk right in. He didn't want to leave his mother's side.

Her heart broke for the young man.

Christina turned the handle and walked in and called up the stairs to announce her arrival. "Hello, it's Dr. Christina." Boxes from moving were still scattered around the foyer. Poor Linda was probably too weak to unpack. Grief sat on Christina's chest. The poor woman might never get to unpack.

Christina took a step toward the stairs and a floor-board creaked. The utter stillness of the home made the flesh on her arms stand up. Suddenly stories of intruders shot by unsuspecting homeowners flashed through her mind. She shook it away. She had been invited to check in on Linda Everett.

The wife of the man you accused of attacking you.

Christina could already imagine Dylan scolding her for going someplace without him. Something deep inside her bristled. She did not need taking care of. Besides, she wasn't taking reckless chances. She knew Roger wasn't around.

Before she lost her nerve, she gripped her doctor's bag in one hand and the railing in the other and made her way up the stairs. About halfway up, she called out again. "Matthew? Linda? It's Dr. Christina. I'm headed up."

Her sweat-slicked palm slid across the railing and she smiled at her ridiculousness. She'd check on Linda and leave. If Linda needed additional care, she'd make sure Dylan came with her next time.

Unfortunately, she couldn't wait for Dylan to return from Buffalo, but she had given him the consideration of a text before she got out of the car in the Everetts' driveway.

The bedroom door at the top of the stairs was ajar. With a hand she couldn't get to stop shaking, she pushed it open. The high-pitched groan of the hinges made icy dread surge through her veins.

Messy sheets were crumpled on the empty bed.

Christina stepped into the room. "Linda?" She hated the shaky quality of her voice.

The bedroom door slammed shut behind her and she jumped. She spun around. Matt stood there blocking the door with a vacant stare in his eyes.

Christina's stomach plummeted to her shoes. "Matthew, where is your mother?"

Matt didn't answer as he took a step toward Christina. She squared her shoulders. She should never have put herself in this position.

"Is your mother home?" Christina asked, this time more forcefully, hoping she could reach the space behind this young man's vacant eyes.

"It's all your fault." His lips peeled back from his teeth.

Christina wavered between peppering the young man with questions and putting her full body weight behind a mad dash for the door. But since the door was behind him, she risked ramming him into the door, which would only make him angry, not provide an escape.

"I don't know what you're talking about." She took a slow step toward him and he didn't budge. "I need to leave. Please get out of my way."

Matthew blinked slowly a few times and she prayed she could reach him.

"My mom and dad have been fighting a lot. My mom's been crying." Darkness flashed in his eyes, reminiscent of the evil she had seen in Roger's eyes the day of her attack.

Christina swallowed hard. "I'm here to help your mom."

"No."

Christina couldn't make sense of her jumbled thoughts.

"I'm a doctor. I'm here to help your mother. I worked with her physicians in Buffalo to find the best treatment to make sure your mom is comfortable."

"I'm not talking about her pain meds, you stupid woman." Matt's fist came out and connected with her jaw so fast, Christina didn't have time to brace herself. It sent her reeling back and she scrambled to catch herself on the edge of the chair, but her wrist folded at an awkward angle and she landed hard on her backside. Then her world went black.

Dylan glanced at his phone, then turned it on silent as he entered his early-morning meeting. His immediate supervisor sat on the other side of the desk and held out a hand.

"Have a seat, Dylan."

Dylan sat down, apprehension coursing through him. He wasn't sure what this meeting was about, but the fact that his supervisor called him in last minute couldn't be good.

"Was there a development in Special Agent Nora Reed's death?" Even saying her name now, the guilt washed over him.

"Yes." His supervisor's reply was curt. He picked up a file on his desk and offered it to Dylan.

Feeling a little light-headed at being back here, about to get the news he'd been dreading for months, he asked, "Can you give me the highlights?"

Surprise registered on his supervisor's face. The older man took the file back and opened it. "Special Agent Nora Reed was not killed as a result of meeting with your CI." The man stopped to let the news sink in.

Since the second he found Nora's lifeless body, Dylan had beaten himself up for sending his partner to her death. To a meeting he should have gone to, but decided she needed the experience. She wanted the experience.

"I don't understand. The CI confessed."

His supervisor shook his head. "The confidential informant had been threatened."

"What?"

"Special Agent Nora Reed's cousin got involved with a violent gang. Somehow the gang leader got wind that his cousin was an FBI agent. They put a bull's-eye on Agent Reed's head. I'm afraid she was a walking target."

"Why didn't we know this? All agents are vetted."

"Yes, but her cousin didn't have a record when Nora applied. For some reason, her cousin went off the rails in a relatively short period of time. Drugs will do that to a person."

Dylan plowed his hand through his hair. "This is crazy."

"The CI was a talker. Word got out that he was meeting with Agent Reed that night. After they killed her, they threatened the CI to keep his mouth shut. I guess he thought it was better to confess to the crime than be out on the streets where the next gang member was likely to put a bullet in his head."

Dylan should have felt relieved. He hadn't led Nora to her death, but somehow knowing about the evil element in the world didn't exactly do anything to give him the warm and fuzzies.

"Why did the CI confess now?"

"He didn't. Nora's cousin came forward. Kid sobered up and remorse got the best of him."

Dylan slumped in his chair, shaking his head. "Unbelievable."

His supervisor closed the folder and clasped his hands on top of it. "How's life in the country? Getting your head back on straight? We really miss you."

Dylan's thoughts wandered to Christina. "Life in the country is pretty good." If he didn't count all the near misses on his life and Christina's.

"Think you'll be ready to come back in January?"

The Bureau believed twelve months would allow him to get over the death of his partner and avoid any more impulsive actions that could put his life or the lives of his fellow agents in jeopardy. He had nearly shot the CI in the head when the frightened teen had raised his hands in surrender. Dylan could only assume it was divine intervention that spared the young CI.

"I should be ready by January."

"Good." His supervisor pushed away from the desk and stood, his way of saying that the meeting was over.

The two men shook hands. Dylan walked out of his supervisor's office and made his way to the lobby. He stepped into the sunshine and, for the first time in a long time, truly enjoyed the feel of the warmth on his face.

His heart ached for Nora's life cut short—that would never change—but a part of him was relieved. He had not sent the probationary special agent to her death. Her drug-addicted cousin had that evil act on his hands.

Dylan reached into his suit-coat pocket and pulled out his phone. He muttered something under his breath when he saw Christina's text.

What was she thinking going to the Everett home alone? He immediately texted Christina right back: How did it go with Linda Everett?

He stared at his phone and a knot slowly tightened in his stomach when he didn't get a response. Did he really think he'd get one immediately? She was probably busy.

Dylan headed back toward Apple Creek. He'd give Christina thirty minutes to answer his text and then he was calling in the cavalry.

FIFTEEN

Christina's head felt heavy as she came around. Matthew must have drugged her. With everything that had been going on she felt oddly calm. Perhaps it was the drugs coursing through her system.

Blinking slowly, she tried to focus despite the blackness surrounding her. She tugged on her arms and legs. Matt had bound her hands together in front of her. Her feet were also bound, but when she wiggled, she felt the ties loosen. She bent forward and worked on the fabric wrapped around her ankles.

If only I can undo this knot.

A disembodied voice floated out from the darkness. "I saw you that night."

Instinctively, Christina sat upright and pressed her ankles together. "What night?" she wanted to say, but her throat was too dry to form the words.

"I was just a kid, but I saw you with my dad. I saw how you were laughing and being silly. Leaning toward him." He paused and Christina imagined him reliving the night at the beach in his mind's eye. "Then something changed and you started running, but my dad was stronger."

He had seen his father attack her on the beach. The

realization hit her hard. Maybe little Matthew had been the reason his father had stopped hurting her. Maybe he had been the reason Christina got away.

"Your father hurt me." Her voice was raspy, dry. She wanted him to focus on the now.

"You did something to make him mad."

Despite the dullness she felt from the drugs, her pulse spiked. "Do you make your father mad? Does he hurt you?"

"We're not talking about me and my dad."

"What your dad did wasn't right."

"My dad's all I have." Matthew's voice cracked.

"You have your mom."

"My mom's going to die," he spit out.

Christina waited a minute, then asked Matthew to turn on a light. Surprisingly, she heard a click and a lone bulb burned in the center of the empty basement. She blinked against the brightness of it.

"I came here today to help your mom. Where is she?"

Half his mouth twitched into a mirthless grin. "She likes to sleep in the back bedroom where she can watch the sunrise. She doesn't sleep much, unless she's heavily sedated."

"Is she heavily sedated now?"

Matthew nodded. He dragged over a stool and straddled it.

"Can you please untie me, Matthew? I won't hurt you."

He jerked his head back. "Don't you see? You already have. Ever since the day you came to our house after the barn party, my parents have been fighting. You need to stay away from my dad. He and my mom were working things out before you came along."

"You have this all wrong. I don't want anything to do with your dad."

"Girls are all the same. They ruin everything."

Christina bit her tongue, figuring Matthew needed to unload everything that was on his chest, weighing him down.

"Cheryl almost ruined everything when she went running to the clinic after Naomi." He shook his head. "Cheryl's the one who stole the drugs from the clinic for me. She's so needy for friends. But she freaked when she heard Naomi was drugged." He swiped a hand across his mouth as if he tasted something bad. "How was I supposed to know Ben was going to rescue Naomi and rush her to the clinic?" He groaned in disbelief. "I heard that one was pretty wild for being Amish. That she did it with townies. I wanted to see for myself. Get a piece of that."

Matthew *was* at the barn party. The realization made her stomach twist.

He'd targeted Naomi. Just like Roger had targeted her when she was in college.

He leaned toward Christina and pointed at her. "I need you to stop ruining my dad's life. My mom doesn't have much time."

"You need to let me go," Christina said softly, trying to appeal to him. "Hurting me isn't going to help anyone."

"You need to pay for ruining my family's lives. I tried to scare you off. Damaging your car, breaking into your home, trying to run you over at the school, but you don't scare easily. You're a fool."

"How did you know we were at the school?"

"I saw you." He gave her a look that read, *Duh*. He drew in a deep breath, as if reliving the moment. "I didn't plan to try to run you over until I saw you—or rather

Dylan—step out from between the buses holding that floral umbrella. You underestimate how observant I am."

The wild look in his eyes panicked her. She had to keep him talking. Find a way out.

"Who do you think alerted the news after we went to the principal with concerns about your father?"

Matt scrubbed his hand across his face, growing agitated. "*That* wasn't me. I was trying to protect my father. Maybe that busybody secretary in the office who always asks a million questions when I show up five minutes late. She's annoying."

Christina suspected they might never know. "You're pretty good at archery," she said, trying to soften him up with flattery.

"Oh, yeah. What did you do? Bend over to tie your shoe? You must have done some good deeds in your past." He shook his head and a slow smile formed on his face. "By all rights, I should have hit you." He pointed to the center of her forehead. "Right there. My dad would have been impressed with that shot." He said it in such a way that Christina suspected his dad rarely expressed pride in his only son.

"You were almost successful out in the orchard. But what would that have solved?"

Matthew started punching his head and wouldn't stop. He was obviously off balance.

"Please, please, stop. I'll help you."

"It's too late."

"It's never too late." She tugged on her restraints. They didn't budge. "What does your father know about all this?"

"I don't think he knows anything about the girl I attacked on campus."

Christina's heart dropped. Matthew had been responsible for that attack, too.

"Maybe he'd be proud of me for that."

"You're not your father. You're your own person." As soon as the words came out of her mouth she wished she could call them back.

"He's not a wimp like me." Matthew shook his head, as if mentally beating himself up.

"Does he know you're into drugs?"

Matthew looked up, as if considering it. "I don't know. I just know he's strong and he won't let you get away with ruining his reputation. You accused him of begin a creep with the girls at my school." Something resembling disgust flickered across his face. "He used the opportunity to turn things around. Hurt you."

"Matthew, you need to stop this now before it goes any further."

Matthew got to his feet and approached her, his face unreadable. "My dad always thought I was a screwup. I'm gonna make him proud of me. I'm gonna show him that I could get you. The one woman he couldn't."

About halfway between Buffalo and Apple Creek, Dylan still hadn't heard from Christina. He called her phone this time and held his breath until her voice mail picked up.

"I'm worried about you. Call me as soon as you get this."

He picked his phone up again and was about to dial Nick, when he threw it back down. He had to trust her. He couldn't go calling the sheriff every time he couldn't get hold of her.

By the time he reached Apple Creek, Dylan decided

to drive directly over to the Everett's house. His heart started racing when he noticed a pickup truck in the driveway. Was that Henry's truck? Had Christina borrowed it?

Dylan parked behind the truck and was already preparing all the excuses he could use when he found Christina unharmed and annoyed with him. He knocked on the front door and waited.

No answer.

He tried the door handle and it was locked. Pulling his gun out of the holster strapped across his chest, he stalked around the house, trying to look in all the windows.

Nothing seemed out of place.

As he walked around the back, he thought he heard muffled voices. Bending, he peeked in the basement window and noticed a lone bulb swinging from the ceiling. He saw Matthew sitting on a stool, but his view of the rest of the basement was obscured.

He knew in his gut that Christina was in trouble.

Dear Lord, please protect her. Guide me in helping her. The prayer came to his mind, surprising him.

When he came around the back, he noticed Dorothy doors leading into the basement. He blinked, stunned at what he was looking at. He couldn't believe it.

Thank you, God.

With one hand tightly wrapped around his gun, he slowly opened the door and cringed at the high-pitched screech the hinges had made. He'd never be able to make a surprise entrance at this rate.

Plowing forward, he descended the steps, blinking as his eyes adjusted to the deep shadows as the light still swung from the ceiling. Someone was obviously nearby.

All of a sudden, Matthew emerged from the shadows,

holding a gun aimed at him. He was pale and shaking. "No, no, no," the young man muttered.

"Take it easy, I'm not going to hurt you. I need to find Christina."

Out of the corner of his eye, he saw motion in the shadows. He wasn't sure if it was a trick of the eye from the swinging lightbulb. But the next thing he knew, Christina had her bound arms raised, holding a two-by-four, and was advancing on Matthew from behind. The teenager went down with one blow, the gun clattering across the cement floor.

Dylan scooped up the gun, then ran for Christina. He wrapped his arm around her, steadying her.

"It's about time you got here," she muttered, then smiled brightly at him, the light from the bare bulb dancing in her eyes.

SIXTEEN

"You're one tough cookie." Dylan rubbed Christina's chafed wrists as they sat at the Everetts' kitchen table. She wanted nothing more than to get out of here, but she knew the sheriff had to do his investigation.

"I'm grateful I was able to undo my ankles while Matthew was hiding in the shadows waiting for you to come down into the basement."

"Yeah, me, too." Dylan smiled.

Christina was still struggling to get her head around the fact that Matthew had been the one terrorizing Apple Creek. Terrorizing her.

She slowly shook her head, still trying to rein in her emotions as her body got rid of the antianxiety meds in her system. "I can't believe it was Matthew. His father must have done a number on him over the years for him to turn out to be so—" she struggled for the right word "—off. I can't believe he was behind the attacks against the young women in this community and then against us."

"His world was spiraling out of control with his mother's illness. He was losing his grasp on reality."

Nick approached with his hat in his hand. "They're

taking Linda to Buffalo to stay with her sister. She'll be closer to her doctors there, too."

"I don't know how she's going to manage. She's so weak as it is," Christina said. Her compassion for this woman had led her right into Matthew's hands, had almost gotten her killed.

"And Roger?" Dylan asked.

"I have a sheriff waiting to pull him over once he gets back into town. He has a lot of questions to answer. Women made reports against him, too, after the news came out. Seems both father and son had issues." He touched his sister's shoulder. "He's finally going to be revealed for who he really is." He paused a second. "He's finally going to pay."

Christina should have felt relief, but instead she felt yucky. "I better go home and rest."

"You need to go to the hospital."

Christina gave her brother a death glare.

"What if I promise to keep an eye on her? Make sure she's okay?" Dylan offered, wrapping his arm gently around her waist.

Nick hesitated. "Guess that's my sister's call."

Christina nodded. "I need to rest in my own bed."

"I'll make sure she's okay," Dylan said as he guided her toward the door. Then he whispered in her ear. "It's all over. Everything's going to be okay."

Christina sat on a chaise near the French doors of her family home, cradling a cup of hot tea in her hands. Franny had fussed over her as soon as Dylan had walked in the door with Christina. He suspected he could leave and Christina would be suitably cared for, but he found he didn't want to.

"How do you feel?"

"A lot better. Thank you." She twisted and set the mug of tea down on the table next to her chair. "I feel horrible for Linda. She's in poor health and now this."

Dylan sat down on the edge of the chaise and touched Christina's foot through the blanket.

"None of this is your fault."

She tilted her head back and snuggled into the plush chaise. "I know it's irrational, but I can't help but think if I hadn't opened old wounds… If I had let the past rest…" She dragged a hand through her hair. "I keep thinking back to the first day I ran into Roger at his house and we argued in the backyard. Matthew was home. He had to have overheard us. It must have sent him over the edge."

"Matthew was already dabbling in drugs. He drugged Naomi. He admitted attacking the young college woman, too. If anything, you brought this nightmare to a close."

"What will happen to Cheryl?" She clasped her hands. "Kids can be so impressionable. In her eagerness to fit in, she stole the drugs from the clinic. I'm guessing she also stole my prescription pad, the one Matthew shredded and left on my bed." She bit her lower lip, as if giving it some thought. "The reason I even had those particular drugs on hand was from when I was treating Nick's mother-in-law before she died. I had them locked up. Cheryl used Naomi to gain access to the clinic."

"I get the sense Cheryl is remorseful."

Christina looked at him in surprise. "Does that matter?"

"Tough to say. Maybe the courts will let her off with a minimal sentence or even probation."

"I'll have to give it some thought on how I want to help her. It still makes me so angry that she betrayed her good friend's trust." Christina stifled a yawn and pulled a blanket up to her shoulders.

Dylan stood. "I'll let you sleep a bit."

Christina reached out her hand and Dylan accepted it. "Sit back down. Please."

Dylan lowered himself onto the chaise. "You never told me about your visit to the FBI headquarters."

A strange calm settled over him. "Apparently my partner was the target of a gang initiation involving her cousin."

Christina pressed her lips together and shook her head.

"Her murder had nothing to do with me sending her to talk to our confidential informant. Not directly. No matter how hard the Bureau works to protect their own, sometimes evil wins."

"God gave us free will. But instead of focusing on that, remember when God came through for us."

Dylan ran the palm of his hand over his jaw, rough with stubble. He was in awe of Christina's faith. He could learn a thing or two from her.

"Look at how you showed up just in time to save me. I don't think I ever thanked you." She blinked up at him with tired eyes.

He felt a smile pulling at the corners of his mouth. "You were well on your way to saving yourself."

"I could have only done so much with my hands tied together."

"You and a two-by-four are a pretty tough combination."

Christina ran her hands over the stitches of the crocheted blanket. "I'm glad you came when you did."

"Me, too." The words he needed to say got jammed in

his throat. Finally he said, "I don't want to think about what life would be like without you in it."

Christina turned her face toward him, a curious look in her eyes. "That's how you feel now, but you have a whole other life you'll be going back to with the FBI. I can see how you thrived on rushing in and saving me. You must be a very good agent. You'd never be happy in Apple Creek and I have no plans on abandoning my clinic."

Dylan fisted his hand and pressed it to his chest. "Boy, you certainly don't go easy on a guy."

"I can't play this game with you. I really enjoy being with you. I'm grateful for you. But I can't risk my heart and then lose you. Again."

Dylan leaned closer and hooked his thumb under her chin. She finally looked up at him. "I won't break your heart. Please have faith in me." He leaned closer, his lips covering hers. She tasted of orange pekoe and lemon.

"We live in two different worlds," she said, her voice lacking in conviction.

"Perhaps we should trust God in helping us find a way."

Christina reached out and grabbed his hand. "I'd like that."

He smiled, his insides warmed. "Me, too."

EPILOGUE

Eight months later...

Christina's eye was drawn to the large window overlooking the golf course at the Apple Creek Country Club. A light snow had been falling all day and now the increasing wind added to the wintery scene.

Dylan leaned in next to her and kissed the top of her head; the feeling of being protected, loved, warmed her heart. "A penny for your thoughts," he said.

"I'm so happy. Everyone we love is in this room."

"I'm glad your parents and younger sister were able to make it to town before the snowstorm."

"Me, too." She giggled. "Looks like Mrs. Greene has my father's ear. She's probably reassuring him that you're a good guy."

"Mrs. Greene has been my champion."

Christina squeezed Dylan's hand. "I'm sorry your dad wasn't able to come."

Dylan kissed her cheek. "You're my family now."

"You might regret that when you're commuting to work in the winter from Apple Creek." Dylan had insisted they live in her cottage versus her suggestion of buying a home midway between Apple Creek and Buffalo. He was finally going back to the FBI after their honeymoon in Florida. If they could fly out in this weather.

"I'll never regret it." Dylan pulled her into an embrace and kissed her neck. "A commute is a small price to pay to have you as my bride."

Christina giggled and a thread of warmth squeezed her heart.

"I'm glad I finally tuned in to God's plan for us. I was so busy trying to achieve things, prove things to myself, prove things to my dad who really never cared…" His voice trailed off. "I'm sorry I was the guy who didn't care who I hurt along the way."

Christina pulled back, planting her hands on his solid chest. "Sometimes the journey isn't as direct as we'd like it to be. But we're here now. This is a happy day, so no more talk of sad things."

"Beautiful wedding," Sarah Jennings, Christina's sister-in-law, said as she approached with little Emma May on her hip. Nick came up behind them. "Nick and I have to leave soon to get this little one down."

Christina kissed Sarah's cheek. "Thank you for coming. *Really.*"

Nick shook Dylan's hand, then also gave his sister a kiss. Then something flashed in her mind. "Did you hear any updates on Cheryl?"

"Can't this wait?" her big brother asked.

"Tell me." She tried to keep the enthusiasm out of her voice.

"Cheryl was given probation. Hopefully she learned her lesson. Peer pressure and the need to be accepted can lead a young person down a dark path."

"I'm so glad."

"I hear Naomi's doing well," Nick said, then paused, looking a little sheepish. "Since we're on the subject."

"Yes, she is," Christina agreed. Naomi had been baptized and married Lloyd Burkholder, after all. "I saw her at the general store last week. She looks genuinely happy."

Nick smiled and a twinkle lit his eyes. "You do, too, sis."

Christina felt her cheeks flush.

"Well, we better go," Nick said. Sarah lifted her hand to wave and the baby mimicked the gesture. They'd all turned to leave when Nick said over his shoulder, "Keep an eye out for my little sister."

"I can keep an eye out for myself," Christina said, as if on autopilot. She was able to breathe easier now that both Roger and his son, Matthew, were in prison. Roger claimed to not know about his son's illegal activities, but Christina had her doubts. Either way, it didn't matter. Other women who had been assaulted by Roger came forward, sealing his fate. It broke her heart every time she thought of young Matthew. She couldn't help but wonder if he would have turned out differently if he had been raised by a better man.

Recently, Linda had passed away and Christina prayed that she now had peace. A tremble coursed through Christina as she dismissed the thoughts, unwilling to let them darken her special day.

"Are you cold?" Dylan slid his arm around Christina's waist and pulled her close and whispered in her ear, "I know you're fully capable of looking out for yourself, but the beauty of marriage is knowing you don't have to."

One more time, Christina scanned the room where all those she loved had gathered. She was not alone. Perhaps she never had been. Despite the distance sometimes, she always had people in her life who loved her. Wanted the best for her. People she should have trusted more in times of darkness.

Christina pivoted and smiled at her new husband. The man she trusted with her entire heart.

God had given them a second chance at love, filling her with joy.

"I love you, Dylan, more than you know."

"I love you, too." He hugged her close. "I love you, too."

* * * * *

Dear Reader,

Thank you for joining me on another adventure in the Amish community that was just a flicker of an idea when I first learned that Harlequin Love Inspired Suspense was looking for new Amish stories a few years ago. It's hard to believe my first sale to Harlequin, a book titled *Plain Pursuit*, has led to a total of five books set in this same community of Apple Creek, NY.

I maintain an updated list of all my titles on my website: AlisonStone.com. Once on my website, you can also sign up for my digital newsletter to stay informed of all my latest releases and writing news.

I enjoy hearing from my readers via email at Alison@AlisonStone.com or via snail mail at

P.O. Box 333
Buffalo, NY 14051

I look forward to hearing from you. I am truly blessed to have such wonderful readers.

Sincerely,

Alison

SPECIAL EXCERPT FROM

Love Inspired
SUSPENSE

*Desert Valley's new police chief must hunt down the
woman terrorizing his town and keep her from hurting
the dog trainer he's coming to care for.*

Read on for an excerpt from
SEARCH AND RESCUE,
the exciting conclusion to the series
ROOKIE K-9 UNIT.

"I'm going to make a quick run to town and back," Sophie
told newly minted police chief Ryder Hayes and noted his
scowl in response.

"Be careful. You may have been a cop once," Ryder
said, "but you're a dog trainer now."

That was a low blow. Sophie clenched her jaw.

"We all have to be on guard," he said. "There's no
telling where Carrie is or whether she's through killing
people."

"I agree with you. I'll keep my eyes open," Sophie
said.

He arched a brow. "Are you carrying?"

"Of course." She patted a flat holster clipped inside the
waist of her jeans. "I won't be out and about for long. I'm
going to the train station to pick up a dog."

"Why didn't you say so in the first place?"

She was still smiling a few minutes later when she
parked at the small railroad station and climbed out of
her official K-9 SUV.

A sparse crowd was beginning to disembark as she approached. She shaded her eyes. *There!* A slim young police cadet had stepped down and turned, tugging on a leash. "Hello! I've been expecting you. I'm Sophie Williams."

"This is Phoenix," the young man said, indicating the silver, black and white Australian shepherd cowering at his feet. "I hope you have better success with him than we did."

She grasped the end of the leash, gave it slack and took several steps back. She politely bade him goodbye, turned and walked away with Phoenix at her side.

"Heel," Sophie ordered.

The dog refused to budge.

She faced him. "What is it, boy? What's scaring you?"

A loud bang echoed a fraction of a second later. Sophie recognized a rifle shot and instinctively ducked.

The dog surged toward her. She opened her arms to accept him just as a second shot was fired. Together they scrambled for safety behind her SUV.

Don't miss
SEARCH AND RESCUE by Valerie Hansen,
available wherever
Love Inspired® Suspense books and ebooks are sold.

www.LoveInspired.com